And the Things We Talked About

Stories

by James Ross Kelly

And the Fires We Talked About

Stories

by James Ross Kelly

Book Design by UnCollected Press
Cover Graphic: 1987 by Ted Barr
American Artist—1939-1997
used by permission of his Estate.
Back Cover: Henry Grier Stanton

UnCollected Press
8320 Main Street, 2nd Floor
Ellicott City, Maryland 21043

For more books by Uncollected Press:
www.therawartreview.com

First Edition 2020—60 copies

ACKNOWLEDGEMENTS:

The following stories first appeared in these publications: "The Other Night at the Log Cabin," *Rogue Valley Weekly War Whoop and Moral Volcano* 1977; "Sufficient unto the Day," *The Sun: a Magazine of Ideas* 1987; "In Eritrea While Vietnam Raged," *Cargo Literary* 2015; "Above Lyman's Riffle," *Fiction Attic* 2015; "Earned Wisdom," *Flash Fiction*, 2018; "Three Day Pass," *Down in the Dirt* 2019; "She Owned a Restaurant up in Bend," *Rue Scribe* 2019; "A Man's Voice," *Rue Scribe* 2019; "A Woman's Voice," *Rue Scribe* 2019; "Now Let Me Tell You This Story," *The Purpled Nail* 2019; "Easter Sunday Afternoon," *Lucky Jefferson* 2019; "Oh, That's a Mad Thing to Look At!" *Rue Scribe* 2020.

This book of stories is a work of fiction. Mostly set in the last three decades of the Twentieth Century, during an era that we figured we'd have everything figured out by now. Although some of them have a form of an autobiography, none of them are. Space and time and a simple past tense have been rearranged to suit the convenience of story narrative. With the exception of public figures—any resemblance to persons living or dead is coincidental. Opinions expressed are those of the characters herein and should not be confused with whatever notion the author may have.

Contents

This book is dedicated to the memory of my good friend, the poet David Lloyd Whited (1950-2015), who, not finding me home left this poem on my Smith-Corona in 1993.

Even the fish stories were out today
And the lies we told were truth one time
Before they cut the hills and butchered out the
Trout pond, all of us good looking clear-eyed boys
All of us searching for the right ax
And wondering if the bait that we had was the bait
Which they were biting on. Times like these
I'm just too busy to get to work
Times like these that the friends and the neighbors
Which we grew up with are telling us the
Summertime, in the wintertime, in the falling rain
Good stories and good kids, each of them good
And the fires we talked about
Are probably still burning up there on
That damn hillside.

A Man's Voice

S HE HANDED IT TO ME THEN, I DUNNO, how I did
it—knew I shouldn't, but I just sliced me a slice of fruit with
the ol' barlow knife while I was looking at a coiled up snake,
who'd been talking to my woman.

Yes, damnit, I know I should have been suspect of a talking
snake. Howsoever, first thing I know, I was making moonshine, skip
and go naked foolin' round til waay after midnight, every-night,
everything seemed clear for a while, but trouble was I ended up havin'
to get-a-job, plus plow the farm and then the woman left, and I had
to take care of the kids too, and keepin' the house from fall'n apart..
No more huntn' and fishin' just makin' mortgage payments for a
farm I had been given free and clear long ago. Before the bank was
even a notion, and it seems like there was a time when there was just
plants and animals and clear blue sky, white clouds and the low and
high blue flint hills and the woman had really just been a part of me
that couldn't no more leave than I could say anything bad about
anything and having kids didn't involve them growing up and killing
each other. Back then I don't ever remember screaming in the middle
of the night either.

Captain Blood

H E HAD BEEN BACK FROM VIETNAM NINE YEARS. One year in a VA Hospital. He didn't talk the first six months. Five years after that, he began coming into the bar. The Captain always had a model airplane. Generally, it was a fighter plane of some form. He'd sit the small plastic replica in front of him and order a beer. He'd play with the airplane a little bit, but generally not in a manner that was obtrusive to anyone really. Although occasionally he would fly an F-4 Phantom II around over his beer.

"More F-4s were shot down, than any other American aircraft in Vietnam!" he'd tell you.

"F-4s saved our asses!" Captain Blood would say.

"F-4s were the last American aircraft to achieve Ace status." The Captain would make sure you knew this.

Sometimes he had other aircraft with similar facts. I remember getting a tour of a B-29 with folding landing gear. The Captain's airship had moving gun turrets and tiny, working bomb bay doors.

Years later, for a time I worked in a VA Hospital, and saw how VA counselors slowly with loving kindness got Vets to respond who were suffering from a deep Post Traumatic Syndrome Disorder, with model airplanes. In the recreation rooms in brand new boxes with good smelling glue and paint, unlimited time, decent chow, long walks on the pleasant VA hospital grounds, and with months, and sometimes years of care, one-on-one care, and group session care. A process of unobtrusively dragging the whole thing out of them would bring some around. Some leaving. Some coming back in three months, with DTs, or strung out on heroin, and given another session. Some like the Captain going home—sort of.

The Captain spent two years in Vietnam, and was a sergeant, had a silver star and a Purple Heart with oak leaf cluster, meaning he'd been wounded more than once. Occasionally, he'd wear these medals and others on his field jacket. With his long hair billowing over his back he'd zoom into the bar in good spirits. He'd leave that way. He never came in without his air support. The Captain never stayed long and never caused trouble.

One afternoon, a fellow bar-fly quipped, and derisively asked, why he, the Captain, grown man that he was, "Still played with model airplanes?"

"We'll be clear," said the Captain with a flourish. He usually never talked about the war.

"The morning after the Tet Offensive, I saw hundreds of NVA lifeless in the wire around our compound that we killed during their attack. After that, I saw friends killed, women killed, and children killed. It was not over when I left. What I did not tell the shrinks at the VA, I will now tell you." he had turned around with his full chest of medals on his field jacket, and with further flourish looked his accuser in the eye.

"I concluded," the Captain said, "that with all the things I had done over there, it would not make any difference what I did here. But now I simply build model airplanes. Would you have it any different?"

Then the Captain buzzed his F-4 over our beer.

Above Lyman's Riffle

THE OLD MAN'S HOUSE WAS FALLING DOWN ten years after his death; twenty-years after, the whole south face of Lyman Mountain and Ernie's place by the Rogue River, was divided up and there were expensive homes built at various river viewpoints, and no notion of Ernest Lyman, was in anyone's mind. However, one year after he'd passed, on a hot August, dusky evening that was beginning to cool, I waited for the red glow down river and Vaux's swifts darted through warm air and willows along the river. Swifts in the day glow off in the west and evening light!

That evening I could see to my right, the hundred-year-old black walnut and cherry orchard across the road, and up the hill the road that would take you to Ernie's hard rock mine, and below the mountain as it turned north, Sam's Creek was trickling in through the willows upstream from where I was standing.

Once I had seen a specimen nugget come out of Sam's Creek, which was as big as your thumb and weighed over an ounce. The nugget had come from a small inner tube dredge, sucking gravel off the bottom of the creek for gold fines that settled after the gravel rattled across a shaker board. The dredger came up with a frogman mask and then showed Jack and I the nugget of that day's find. Ernie let the guy, Jack's friend, dredge the creek. The man had tried to offer Ernie half of what gold he dredged. Ernie waved him off, despite living in the old falling-down house; he'd invested well and had no need for money.

This evening, in front of Ernie's house, I'm watching the brick chimney, that juts upward from its tin roof at the bottom of Lyman Mountain. Ernie's parents built the house when he was four in 1900, when their gold mine began to pay. He was born across the road not far from where Ernie let me tear an old apple packing shed down two years before his death. The apple orchard had been gone since shortly after the Second World War. The shed was full of early twentieth-century artifacts, a "Coolerator," with only three bullet holes in it—I took the old upright icebox home and kept food in it on the porch in the winter, and would throw in a block of ice in the summer and it would cool beer for three days, despite the bullet holes.

As the packing house deconstructed, behind the siding on the inside wall, written in penciled-in childlike scrawl, an adolescent scribe from 100 years ago had written, "Amen, Brother Ben, shot at a Rooster and hit a hen!" Later, from a ladder, I sided my house with those old Douglas fir lap boards, which were brown and richly weathered with reds, and gray and gold hues—while my own children, my real wealth, squealed and ran across my own side hill seven miles away.

That years ago, evening, the Table Rock Blacktail deer were waiting for the near darkness of after dusk for a drink of river. Then the swifts begin to draw close. For one minute, they came together in ever tightening circles, closer and closer together. Then as one— they swirl into a whirling black-funnel-down-cloud fifty feet in height above the house; and then they are into-the-chimney—in one second, or two.

This vision is what I had waited for, and *suddenly* it had happened, as it did every year, until the chimney fell. The little birds came on a good number of late August and early September evenings before they headed south. I'd watched it before with Ernie, and the old man said they'd used the chimney every summer as long as he could remember. This was the last time I saw this.

An hour before, I had taken a ten-pound summer steelhead trout in the riffle above the falls, on a wet fly, a Teeter's Weighted-Woolly-Worm. Ernie had told me ten years before—it was an evening riffle.

Oh, That's A Mad Thing to Look At!

JOHN MONROE LIVED ON LOST CREEK BY THE COVERED BRIDGE. John ran cattle for decades and always wore a big cowboy hat, John rode roundup in the fall with Leonard Bradshaw. John would hunt mountain lions with Tom Tibbetts as they both kept hounds. Tom said John was the best lion hunter in the county. Tom said they'd start off together and split apart in opposite directions so their hounds would not get mixed up during the chase. The bounties on the big cats every winter, increased the family income, as the lions brought $50 from the state, and $10 from Jackson County, and each successful hunt protected their livestock.

John would not have electricity in his home until a short time after a man walked on the moon. He then gave in to his wife and got electricity and a modern phone. They'd had a crank phone for a time, when Lloyd and his brother were kids. In 94 years, John, had only been to Medford which was 24 miles away—six times.

Once, John's sister decided to take him to the ocean in a car. They were gone for three days. John saw the Redwoods and went to the beach.

Everyone had a distinct cattle call; each owner's beasts knew their master's call. Many of the neighbors knew each other's call. According to Emil Pech, John's call was a good one, with a "Whoopee!" on the end of it.

John gave up on horses when he got old and drove an International Diesel tractor. John was up the South Fork looking for cows and didn't make it back one evening. Lloyd, John's son, went looking for John with his brother-in-law. After finding the tractor at the bottom of a steep grade that went up to Conde Creek, they began calling out for John in the dark, pretty far up the South Fork of Little Butte Creek and up on Hepsie Mountain, past Grizzly Canyon.

Eventually they heard his "Whoopee!" and followed his call in the dark about a half mile from the tractor. He was cold, wet, and muddy and had the big hat pulled over his ears with a plastic sack tied round his head to hold it down. Each of the men got a shoulder under the old cowboy and got him off the mountain.

"I think I had a stroke," John said to Lloyd on the way home in the car, long after midnight.

A few weeks later, John fell while feeding yearling calves. The calves tromped the old man until he crawled under a flatbed wagon, he hauled the baled hay on.

For a brief time, they put him in a nursing home in Medford. John became so sorrowful because he was embarrassed when they took his clothes away. One day, he found his overalls and his flannel shirt and made a break for it out of the nursing home. After that escape, his sons took him home and cared for him there. At the age of 94 John passed, three months after his wife Ida Marie had died. Lloyd said, John would say of his one trip to the ocean:

"Oh, that's a mad thing to look at! That's a mad thing—those waves coming in!"

Surely Goodness and Mercy

FROM A LITTLE FURTHER UP PEPPER CREEK ROAD, on the knob that was the Bingham's place, the circumstances wouldn't have seemed much: a beat-up blue pickup stopping on a dirt road; the somewhat odd sight of a cowboy jumping up and down and waving his arms beside the pickup for less than two minutes; then, the truck slowly leaving the cowboy and driving up the road with more dust trailing behind as it picked up speed.

It was however, that Richard Long had been driving up Pepper Creek Road ten minutes after Andy Pearce had found one of his father's registered Hereford cows, belly-up dead and heart-shot in the middle of their lower pasture that ran along Pepper Creek before it ran into Butte Creek. Andy had seen Long's truck coming and stepped over the leaning barbed wire fence, then leapt out into the road in front of Long's pickup. Over time Richard Long had several confrontations with Andy's family through the years they'd all lived along Pepper Creek—which was virtually all of everyone's lives, their fathers and grandfathers lives—and each of these fully armed stressful encounters was on the subject of hunting rights.

Richard Long felt he had the right to hunt anywhere the deer and elk were, where his father and his father's father had shown him where to hunt, and those places he'd found on his own. The game and nature did not acknowledge straight lines of fences, nor the common-law definition of property lines, nor the legal penalty for trespass. This was how man had hunted this area for all but the most very recent, and thinly sliced segment of the great pie of time.

Andy's family felt their property rights were sacred even though they'd over logged and overgrazed the 5,000-acre ranch for fifty years. Andy's grandfather had bought six different family farms, razed the homes, and consolidated his holdings during the depression. The steelhead and Coho salmon no longer ran up Pepper

Creek that Andy's grandfather had dammed to irrigate their hay fields almost fifty years ago. It was also a fact that their family took a little more than their share of venison every year from the herds that migrated through their ranch in the late autumn.

They'd tried to throw Richard off the steep and remote corners of their land which bordered federal land a half dozen times. Each time, Richard would say something rotten about large parcels of land being locked up by private ownership and Richard would often as not call Andy's father a son-of-a-bitch or something worse, and then he'd keep walking through their land. The younger Pearce a few years back, when he was in his early adolescence, had witnessed one of these incidents and secretly was ashamed at his father's wise decision just to let it go with words. When Andy's mother tried to throw Richard off their land Long had just kept walking.

There were five other large corporate ranches in the area; the Pearce's Rocking C was the only family-run operation left. All the corporate ranches had the same problem with Long and had their company cowboys out looking for Richard every hunting season. Despite this, no one had ever successfully thrown Richard Long off of anywhere.

Richard Long (no one ever called him Dick), was six-foot eight and weighed 240 pounds. In 1974, Richard had written Mohammed Ali a letter, shortly after the heavyweight champion had beaten George Foreman to regain his title in Zaire. The letter allowed as to how Richard knew he'd never get the chance, but nonetheless, Long wrote the boxer, he was positive he could kick his ass.

"Respectfully Yours, Richard Long," the letter had ended.

Richard did not kill the Pearce's prize Hereford cow that was in the middle of the pasture with its feet sticking up in the air. The heinous deed had been done by the resident of a trailer park from twenty miles away, who had murdered the animal the night before, during a beer-drinking-spotlighting-Friday-night-killing spree the second week of deer season.

The initial dialog with Long, where the younger Pearce had alleged, to his face, that it was Richard Long who shot the beast, had been almost unintelligible. The words somewhat slurred, came from underneath Pearce's $200 cowboy hat that sat atop his beet red face with the Copenhagen chewing tobacco uncontrollably flying out of the young man's mouth between the syllables of the words through which he was trying to assert his family's property rights and his genuine grief for the cow.

Richard had initially started to feel sorry for the young man who had just lost his cow. Perhaps he somehow sensed underneath the bravado, he had been attached to the large animal as if it were a monstrous pet and its dead hulk was quite visible just off to their right. When the accusation had finally gotten around to sinking in around the yelling and jumping, Richard Long hadn't even gotten mad.

But when Pearce had turned around and ran to his pickup, fished around behind the seat and then ran back toward Long with a pistol in his hand—Richard's stare became wrought iron and expressionless. Andy was out of breath by the time he'd stood again in front of the drivers' door and held the .357 magnum out at arm's length and pointed at Richard's face.

"Long, God damn you!" Pearce shouted. "You son-of-a-bitch! You think you can get away with anything you want to because you're such a big son-of-a-bitch! Now YOU ain't going to anymore!"

Long continued his stare into the young man's bulging eyes, then pulled the loaded, bolt-action .300 Winchester Magnum rifle sitting beside him on the pickup seat, by the barrel and made it appear out the window almost instantaneously pointed at Andy's chest.

"If that's the way you want 'er," Richard said, having clicked the safety off with his right thumb, as the young man continued to tremble.

Andy's shaking was initially not from fear, but from his own rage. Now they had become the same thing. Pearce made a series of whistling noises through his clenched teeth with saliva coming out with little specks of black tobacco chew, and he then lowered the handgun down to his side. Immediately as he did so, Long clicked the rifle back on safe and pulled the weapon back through the window. The boy would not look at Long but stared at the ground to the left of his own feet.

"Sorry 'bout your cow," Richard Long said.

He looked at the young man for the last time, then made the blue pickup clunk into second gear. The pickup started its wheels rolling up the winding dirt road past Pearce's ranch and on up Pepper Creek toward higher elevation. There the deer were beginning to move and there was the crisp smell of fall in the air, mingled with that morning's essence of oak, sugar pine and Douglas fir wafting through the open windows of the pickup with a rawness of the gravel road.

The deer and elk were gaining the last layer of fat with the good browse of black oak acorns, Idaho fescue, ceanothus, elk sedge, manzanita and willow before the coming snow would cover everything in frozen whiteness three weeks from that moment. Mercy was riding somewhere over the shoulders of the driver and the man left standing back down the road. Goodness surrounded them both.

Standing in the Rain

HE STARTED WRITING NOVELS BECAUSE TOM ROBBINS PISSED HIM OFF and Hemingway had been dead for twenty-three years. I'll spare you the math, this was 1984. Working five-to-midnight shifts at a Eugene, Oregon photo lab allowed for time to write. And it allowed as well, for three to four shots of Meyers with a couple of beers at a convenient bar after work before he would head back across the street and into an alleyway that led quietly to his one-bedroom, bottom floor duplex that gave off its puke hue in the city light. Disjunct in the perpetual ugly twilight of the mercury vapor streetlight glowered, as if something was going on out there in front, the yellow clapboard house whose shadow left him insecure as he fumbled for his keys under the darkness of his own porch light that burned out some nine months ago.

He turned on the lamp by the door as he entered, and the reflections off the fifty-dollar used color TV, that sat inert atop a nondescript coffee table, partially lit up with the patterns of the old Belgian carpet in the Goodwill and Salvation Army furnished apartment. He walked to the breakfast nook that came off the kitchen counter, switched on a desk lamp that hung over the table, then reached to the other side of the Smith-Corona electric typewriter, and turned it on to a comforting hum.

He looked at his name typed in caps at the right-hand corner: ABEL WEST. He then punched the carriage return a couple times to hear the sound and effect, as much as he wanted to look over the words he'd left off with. Abe was working on his third novel. He had left off in the middle of one of his protagonist's many affairs that plagued him through an enigma of the past decade by episodes of drug abuse, sometimes colorful alcoholism, and sex. Most of it was nothing like Abe's life, or at least the exploits in his novels were ones that had never really worked out in Abe's life.

He sat down at the typer and through a few sentences got back a rhythm of language that he had left off with the night before, a rhythm that had become automatic recently. The rhythm became one with the typewriter keys and he was off. A little word craft, with backspacing and some "Wite-out" then a blast or two of stream of consciousness for a couple sentences, then a slow peck of writing it down. It felt good.

John Cain Monroe was a private detective who began his shamus career after a ten-year stint with the Portland, Oregon police department, shortly after a year in Vietnam and a college degree from the GI Bill. He'd left being a police officer the night after he'd found out two of his colleagues had thrown bums off the Burnside bridge just because they had suffered some mild verbal abuse, and mostly just because they could. Monroe had had friendly banter with the homeless men the afternoon of their murder. But this was all in the first novel. West had liberally based the cop part of the character on a guy he'd worked with at the photo lab and who had been a cop and had told him most of these stories. Abe had shown him some of the work and he was amused, mostly by the antics that Abe had woven into his life that was nothing like his life as a supervisor in a photo lab.

When he'd left police work, Abe's buddy like Monroe, had been ready to go for some time anyway. The cops were all carrying "throw away" Saturday night special pistols strapped to their ankles in case they shot someone by mistake. It seemed to him every month somebody got shot by mistake. Like his real-life counterpart, Monroe became a cop to impress his in-laws just before he got married right after taking a BA with a couple criminology courses, and six months as an MP in the military. The marriage had lasted two years, and his wife ran off with a lawyer who, of course made, a lot more money than John would ever have being a Cop. Again, I digress that was in the first novel as well.

John C. Monroe was a Vietnam Veteran. He thrived on bars and vitriolic one-night stands looking for some elusive justification that hadn't ever seemed to develop, as he solved case after case—and Abe had thrown-in a couple he did not solve to create an enigma that made Monroe a solid man with flaws. After the first hundred pages of the first novel, Monroe the Shamus, began to solve crime and bed beautiful women. This moved him through one woman after another who appeared in succession with each caper: a murder, then the solution, the bedding of the babe, and then the misplaced notion of felonious intent in the story arc and John Cane Monroe helping the client out of the tight action and rock solid alibis, and Monroe usually walking away from anything that carried more for the client than five years. Except his clients who were evenly divided as guilty and innocent seldom fell into trouble worth more than five years. Abe allowed about 7,000 words for each segment; and they connected variously, and he made sure some of them stood as stories in themselves. The women were loose versions of wives, girlfriends, or secretaries of the clients. Abe made Monroe not particular: he was writing to sell, and he could smell success at about 200 pages into the first novel.

Abe was now writing his third novel and was thirty pages into a tall red head that had, heretofore, been the most enigmatic character of them all. He liked her, had John C. Monroe liking her, and had now put her in the position of going back to her husband and leaving his hero in the lurch— the goodbye lingered as they both stood in the rain. After a gushy kiss that Abe had loosely ripped off without plagiarizing from a description in a dopy romance novel he found in the trash, he made Monroe slowly let go and pushed her away and did an about face, to walk down a half-lit alleyway and the chapter was about over. He liked the ending but felt a little shallow in that perhaps he was creating a dopy detective novel instead. Then again, a dopey detective novel that sold was fine. Moving the man through the fictional world was his job and he just as quickly dashed his second thoughts and got Monroe set up for another episode.

She had taken old John for a ride. They had all taken John for a ride. But Monroe was always getting in the car and leaving on top of the game with his existential angst, and Abe always had John Monroe keeping his sense of humor, as he bedded women that were mostly always out of his financial league, and Monroe always gave them the chance to be an exception. Each chapter began and ended with glib, sardonic one-liners that hit the solar plexus somewhere between laughter and tacky suicidal angst. Abel, with care and art however, up to this time had kept each ending from being either contrite or cliché. Monroe was a gentleman as well. He never pursued the women, he never kissed them unless they leaned in and wanted to be kissed, and he never made a tawdry, awkward move toward them. There was always a feeling, a touch by them, on his arm, or hand, or faraway eyes, and then a touch, but always a first touch by the women.

Abel West's hero had been wading his way through this for a decade in the three books he had written; and, some of the women had been thinly disguised versions of women whom Abe himself had known and slept with, courted, run away from, admired, wanted to marry, or who wouldn't give him the time of day. He had preserved mannerisms if not their appearances and had some of them to a descriptively precise portrayal of enigmatic behavior which might read through to anyone familiar with these women. On the other hand, no one familiar with these women read detective novels. This was all wrapped around a simple story arc that resembled a hint of Raymond Chandler-like existential description through his protagonists' eye. Abe knew he was not nearly as good as Chandler and left it at that—no one was as good as Chandler. It was good enough that his cheesy detective stories were selling.

John C. Monroe was not an antihero; however, his redemption was a matter of fact, and he carried it like he was the driver of a fast car. Abe thought any notion of needing it explained distracted from the sex and violence that sold. Monroe always carried his ethics and morality on his sleeve, but in the moment, he would sleep with a man's wife if he was not a friend, until it became complicated. He would always clean out a dead man's wallet of cash before the cops came. It was always clear to the reader that Monroe was not a cop, though he had been one. He didn't take bribes; he had clients that paid him fees—more than once he had remarked to himself that there was only a slight difference. This difference blurred a little, but in each story, Abe had uncovered evil that had prevailed for a time, then it was exposed and impaled for all to see with a couple exceptions that left the reader and the characters perplexed.

Disclaimers were always on the frontispiece to keep publishers out of court if someone did not like the resemblance; this gave Abe the comfort of going up to the line in using human behavior that he'd witnessed as material because some of it was better than anyone's creative effort could invent.

Monroe's demeanor was ever contrite, and all his exploits had flowed out onto the paper rolled into the Smith Corona, to a sometimes very surprised Abel West. The existential romance and the myriad of women: was this a misogynist? Perhaps so, Abe disliked feminists of most stripes and didn't care. He was not writing this fiction for any of these women who he considered most as characters from Orwell's sex police. So, every once in a while, he wove one into his narrative as well. Abe's notion of the whole matter was simple: men were violent, and women generally were not, in the physical realm. Their use of sex as a violent tool however, Abe contended, as portrayed well through Monroe's exploits, made it apparent that women could be bloodthirsty gladiators that laid a wake of misery behind them like an SS Panzer division. And it generally began with a smile. Some women in Abe's life had been portals to hell —that he had at least peered into. Then again, Abe took care to portray a plethora of women with motivations ranging from Madonna the mother of God, to Madonna the banshee rock star.

Abe had built John's character, as a man who no matter what provocation ensued, would never hit a woman. Except for the few times these women pulled guns on him, the one who had bit him and drawn blood, and the three times he'd been stabbed—then he popped them a good one each time. Monroe was a martial artist and loved to take weapons away from people in close proximity. Nothing really deviated from these ethics in the course of Abe's writing.

Mostly, he had them down to John ravishing their bodies in between the good Detective stuff, and he would disparage their characters because many of them were disparageable. The couple of saint-like mothers he'd saved and restored were the notable exceptions. Abe had rare chapters however where some old man, or an orphan would need his help.

Having Monroe fall in love and get married though, would have ended the tough guy formula—and the line of his books. So, the good juicy stuff that was well laced with enough sex to keep the formula going had to stay. Settling down to true love and romance always had to go.

This formula was not without success. In addition to his first two pulp fiction thrillers, Abe had sold a chapter of each to *Penthouse* and *Playboy* magazine. He submitted them without changes, and they seemed to fit right into the short story genre, breadth, and plot formation, that though standard, had turns in it to have twisted checks out of both New York and Chicago and into his then severely sparse bank account.

These publication triumphs were a huge coup for Abel West which got him an advance on his royalties for the book he was working on: after the publisher saw his first twelve chapters he offered Abe an advance that made his heart surge and he signed the publication deal right away. Abe had only to finish the book and send it off for another royalty advance; they liked it; and they would publish within three months. And they offered him a contract for three more books.

That these were not much different than romance novels had occurred to Abe in the beginning. Now however, the *Playboy/Penthouse* success had dispelled this notion. He thought he'd put enough existential torment into his fiction in a manner that he thought was legitimately beyond that—the magazine coup kind of clenched this notion except for the one lousy review that accused him of latent misogyny. He smirked when he read it and banished it from his thoughts. Jesus, he'd been published in Penthouse, of course someone would write that! On the other hand, Abe did like to write about tits. He liked to go over the real estate and describe mammary glands, as an advocate for a species of mammals, as he described it. And *Playboy/Penthouse* magazines had been his research text books. Breasts were the primary thing, and the first thing, and after the first thing, was the other first thing—Beauty. The Beauty of a face, the first thing you see, and call it wordlessly beautiful and smile. The notion of misogyny as party plank of feminist ideology from that standpoint, it would jujitsu into a selling point. So, he loved the disparaging review. There would be no bad press here as he saw it. He'd never been writing for feminists, or their fellow travelers. Abandon all ideology was part of his, and John C. Monroe's credo— because as he saw it, any ideology can fuck you up in the end.

The women that Abe had made up had been either goddess or whore, or a little of both. And the current redhead that he had completely made up was one of the former. She was unlike the others completely: classically beautiful—a *noir* Hedy Lamar, Delilah on wheels. Abe tapped nervously with the space bar and stretched the keys all the way out to the bell then got up to heat what was left of yesterday's steak casserole in the microwave.

Then back from turning on the humming device, he again got in touch with typer keys and yesterday's language and began blending out of the right side of his brain. He was in Monroe's emotions and had his guts turning over, feeling all the old psychic wounds come back as the redheaded woman's departure seemed to draw near. All the wounds he had seemed to heal in the course of the last three chapters were popping out on the paper for Abe as he wore Monroe's anxiety on his sleeve describing the Detective's thought life.

John Monroe was becoming a likeable happy guy, but Abe West had ground for him to cover. So, in a page and a half she was at her end in the tale, having planned her and Monroe's relationship after a tidy divorce from her physician husband, and it was all building up to this one line that Abe was stretching for. Because he liked her, he had a notion she might come back in another episode or even in the next book. The tidiness of a divorce and the connubial status of her and Monroe did not fit with the character he'd created. So, John was simply dumping her with a "get your shit together babe, then give me a call some time." Life and literature, or an attempt at literature, should be that simple. He was plumbing the depths of his character to come up with this line, but it was not coming seamlessly.

This was the point when the junkies upstairs had put on a Lou Reed album at top volume making the ceiling vibrate to a dull bass thud of muted lyrics to the over and-over-again-rhythm and Abel lost the one line comeback that was about to standardly round out the chapter. Though it was still two sentences away, it had started the process of marching from one side of Abe's brain to the other and then hopefully to the typewriter keys but had disappeared in one synaptic pause of attention. The microwave bell rang.

Abel started eating the casserole he dumped into a bowl. The coffee was still hot. And so was West as for the hundredth time in the last three months he began banging on the ceiling with a broom handle, and as flakes of plaster had just settled to the floor, then predictably the music from the junkies upstairs receded to an imperceptible drone.

He poured his coffee and walked back to the typer, but that perfect line was gone. He thought it would come back if he pushed it, but it seemed useless after a couple minutes. He sat down and read through the last lines of the manuscript, a few changes with a fine tipped black pen above the double-spaced lines of words, then he gave up, drilled the platin down to the last line, turned the Smith-Corona off and turned the television on.

The tube cracked and squeezed out a small white dot and brought the audio portion of the signal. While it warmed up, Abel West was looking out the window. It was raining a small drizzle that pecked against the window by the couch he had settled into.

James Garner appeared on the screen in his inimitable P.I. role, a rerun episode he'd seen before. He was tempted to watch it, taking to task the tough, well-meaning character and his predictably plotted troubles of every week over and over again, he turned it off without being further tempted to change the channel and went back to the typer. He liked James Garner. Perhaps John Cain Monroe owed his existence to James Garner, but John Monroe got laid regularly, Abe saw to that.

Walking across the room and just before he turned the typer on the one-liner came back, and John Monroe left the redhead, the Doctor's wife, standing in the rain much chagrined. As true romance it had all been less than fair, but Monroe's credo was always, "No one ever handed anybody a ticket in this world saying it was gonna be fair, because ten out of ten men died."

He poured the last bit of his pint of Meyers into the last of the coffee and cranked the paper out of the Smith-Corona, put it face down into the cardboard box and felt good. Chapter twenty-three done and in the can. Why it had taken this long to do something he always knew he could do was not quite a mystery, but to himself a justification for all the years of wanting to be a writer. Now it was happening. He was writing every day and he was not going to let it stop.

Yes, Abel West was on a roll and had come up with something after he'd weathered through the years of rejection slips— namely it was a little luck and lot of discipline(he wrote every day) or maybe it was the fear that he didn't have much time left, or maybe they are the same thing. Abe was nearing forty and it didn't seem like a big deal, he knew the lazy damn attitude of his writing habits from a decade ago were a thing of the past. Abe wrote every day.

Abel West felt good. Almost as good as when the third chapter of his first novel had been accepted as a short story by *Penthouse*. And why the hell not? It had been a long dry decade. West thought it one of those flukes of deserved good luck that happens along. But he was on a roll and had sent the first 10 chapters to three different publishers and had received replies from two of them saying yes they liked the work; but no, they would not give an advance from a sparsely published author; and yes, they would like to see the manuscript upon completion; and no, they did not think publication of one of the chapters in a national magazine would present a problem. Then the paperback shill pulp fiction company that had published his first two novels with no advance and a measly 6% royalty (which really meant mostly no money), called him and offered an advance on the current novel he was working on, and upped the royalty on his first two novels retroactively to 12%. This meant Abe had $5,000 coming if he'd sign a contract. Abe signed the contract. The first two books had started to sell after the magazine success. The larger publishers could kiss his ass—it was working.

It hadn't gone to his head either. He'd been making it home every night to crank out more and more. He had begun to zero in on what it was that he thought of as, "almost success"; if it was pulp fiction, so be it. He'd begun to see it as a ripening, maybe long overdue but a ripening, nonetheless. Abe kept his job at the photo lab because it was an easy seven-hour gig. He sold the old '64 Chrysler and bought a four year old four-wheel drive pickup from one of the Japanese companies, that got three times the mileage the old Chrysler had been getting, and it had the ability to cruise up and down I-5 at a high rate of speed. He'd blasted up to the Puget Sound and spent the weekend fishing off a pier with his poet buddy and drinking rum and brandy mixed up, and they called it "Randy." One night this made two English girls that happened by to inspect their fish bucket giggle when Abe or Dave offered them some "Randy." After about ten minutes of this the two women had to confide to them that "Randy" meant Horny before they left laughing down the pier. That night they had caught several nice true Cod that Abel still had in the freezer. Earlier in the fall Abe went to Southern Oregon and hunted deer and had some venison still in the freezer. Abel West was a paperback writer and felt good. The money made from writing entirely paid for his recreation; and now the upcoming layoff from the Photo lab might heretofore mean the day job had become unnecessary.

Playboy had published a chapter that he'd written as a story complete in itself, about one of the real women in his life— a woman who had for three successive years turned his life upside down, left him, come back, left him again, come back again; each time telling how important it was to have babies with him, left again only to come back pregnant not knowing exactly who the father was, and after he said he didn't care, she left him again to have an abortion. Then she came back and left him again! The success in *Playboy* came largely from three helpful reviews his second novel received after the magazine story. Yes, and a little of it was revenge, mostly aimed at his own stupidity. It was all infinitely worse than how he'd fictionalized it. Yet, Abe was writing every day.

So, Abel West felt good, and thought he should feel good. There was soon to be a new pulse of $5,000 dollars in the bank account, and on the horizon, it seemed he could be entirely supporting himself with his brand of pulp fiction.

In years past he knew the money would go quickly in some form of self-imposed dysfunction in his life, but now there was just the stolid inertia that was sometimes just a banal attempt to keep cranking it out. He'd written hundreds of one-pagers that lingered in a dusty cardboard box, the sides bent from many successive moves. And yes, now by damn he was in his late thirties, and it was beginning to roll.

He was just finishing the last of the Meyers and coffee when the doorbell rang as he sat on the couch watching the smoke roll up from his Camel straight cigarette, then it rang again in quick succession. He got up without thinking about who it could be at 3:30 a.m. opened the door to drizzling rain and a woman standing wet and immediately in front of him. A woman he'd never seen before.

"YOU!—SON-OF-A-BITCH!" she screamed and pushed her way past him to the Belgian carpet in the middle of the room. She stood dripping on the many patterns of the rug with her back to him. This was strange, but many strange things had happened to Abe in this neighborhood, the place gave rise to almost any number of different sets of possibilities. He didn't know this woman and prepared for some kind of bout with the insane, subnormal, and confused, which from time to time seemed to claim Abe as a part and parcel, of a vague wave of humanity.

She just stood there dripping with her back to him, fishing in her purse and turned her profile toward him as she found a long-filtered cigarette and proceeded to light it. Still no memory clicked in of anyone Abe had ever known.

"Look, you're in the wrong apartment," he said gently.

She turned back toward the wall above the television, and then with a high heeled about face, spun around and hit Abel West on the jaw knocking him back and almost down.

"FUCK YOU!" she screamed. "YOU ARE ONE NO GOOD, BASTARD, ASSHOLE, PRICK!"

The junkies began jumping up and down on the floor upstairs; Abe knew now that whatever this was, it was trouble. He stood rubbing his jaw and looking at this redhaired, wet woman in his living room and figuring that he wouldn't let her hit him again.

She began walking around in a tight circle in front of him with arms crossed over medium but ample sized breasts and still smoking, but now in hurried little puffs.

"You left me there," she said, her tone was almost calm now.

"You left me there," she repeated, "in the rain with that son-of-a-bitch of yours turning his back on me for good!"

West was incredulous. The years of trying desperately to grip reality was going out the window. This could not be, but it did seem to be Stella—Stella of the last chapter, red hair and yes, green eyes and a mole slightly over the corner of her mouth and standing there looking at him her head bobbing up and down. It was her right down to the gold lamé handbag he'd outfitted her with. Right down to her cleavage with the beauty mark right center of her breastbone and the bloom of her emerging breasts riding side by side, and right down to all of her great beauty. As skeptical as Abe was, he was more astonished at her beauty.

"YOU'RE FUCKING RIGHT, I'm STELLA!" she yelled presciently. The junkies banged on the floor again overhead to belie this fictitious voice not having an effect.

"You left me there with that stupid one-liner coming out of his mouth, what was it?

"BABY," she distorted her voice to a bass drawl,

"YOU'LL LIVE THE REST OF YOUR LIFE WITH THIS ONE REGRET," what the fuck kind of soap opera crap is that? And then he walks off into the rain leaving me standing there. You thought you were done with me. WELL YOU'RE NOT FUCKING DONE WITH ME!" she screamed.

Abe thought that this couldn't be happening; he hadn't done hallucinogenic drugs in years. There was too much about all of this for it to be a dream. Stella? God could it be? Ah, it *was* Stella but wait, wait a minute! Somebody must be reading his manuscript, and this was a joke, he thought. They came in here in the afternoon, read the manuscript, found this babe to come over here with this great act— ha! That's pretty good. Except for the fact that he really didn't have friends in Eugene and what she was talking about, he had *just* written. People had begun to leave him alone. He'd moved around so much in the last four years that there hadn't been anyone close enough to pull something off like this.

"THIS," she screamed prophetically as she hit him again, "…IS NOT ACTING! THIS IS PISSED!" He was totally off his guard this time and Abe went down.

She threw herself down on the couch and began to sob and rolled herself up into a fetal position. Abe slowly got up off the floor, again rubbing his jaw. He hadn't really been hit since high school and it hurt. He stood there watching her cry and somehow that hurt as well.

"Hey, I, uhm…," he began—but he didn't get very far.

"Do you think," she asked between sobs, "I was really going back to that ass for brains Doctor husband of mine for good? No matter how much money he had? Am I one of the shallow-brained bitches that you dragged up on the previous pages? How can you be such a hack to pull off such a cheap shot as having him leave me in that alleyway? Leaving me there hanging in the middle of a tough guy platitude? You understood that I loved him! I love him!" she moaned.

Abe now felt bad. This was getting to be too much. He had to be incredulous and accepted that it was a real person in front of him, even if it was, he, himself that had created her. And yes, *this* was impossible.

"And where do you get the nerve to pull the plug like that?" she said, "...Your cute little formula writing dragging me in with all of those other bitches while your Mr. Cool, poor baby, Nam vet existential blues boy, sometime PTSD son-of-a-bitch, walks away from me in the rain..."

"I loved him, I loved him hard, but we had to put some space in it, I had to deal with the marriage. I just couldn't cut it off like that, and he had a lot of things to get together. You have to bring me back!

"AND YOU spend thirty pages getting him to let it all work out, for a change. Dissolve all of his insecurities on my bed, then PFFT! he's gone! Off to another adventure with your sick fucking mind. And me, the only thing that has made him seem human in all your stinking chapters has been me! ME! GOD DAMN IT! Because I really love him!"

Abe knew she had him there, it was true. Everything he'd written before Stella was rote, sex, drugs, violence, rock-and-roll one piece of tripping anxiety after another, but no sympathetic women characters—save Stella. There was always a little humanity about Monroe, the character who could be loved, and this could have been wooden, except Abe had done this in a likeable sort of way, with one-liners at just the right time, and a tempo that led to them but didn't give that away; and he was content for that to be his art. Stella was a sympathetic female, and she was the only one he had ever come up with. He was not particularly proud of this, but up to now this had not fazed him.

"Leaving ME out?" she pleaded. "And you, your damn short declarative sentences and your just short of, and sometimes soft pornographic descriptions, you publicly ravaged every part of my body, described every move I made in bed for untold thousands of creeps out there to jerk off to! You put me through this humiliation and then you leave me in the rain as if I was another one of your shallow foolish women with their cocaine eyes and addled brains, that you have happened to pick up in bars and then write on paper as much for your own inadequacy as theirs! And, YOU! who have not been able to keep a woman because you've pissed your life away in bars until recently, with your part-time short-term jobs just enough to get by on, so you can write, but never make enough take a girl out to dinner more than once every three months?"

Abe thought that this was hitting low, and though he was in a state of incredulity it seemed that she was coming on with an eerie prescience he didn't like. After all he had an advance on this sleazy novel and a modicum of success was coming his way, he'd paid off most all of his bills with the first two novels and sent his eighty-year-old pops a thousand bucks. He was only really working because it was part of the routine that worked. He had two royalty checks arriving every month as the first two novels were selling, they were not "Best" selling but they were selling—and paid the rent and bought all his groceries. And, damn it he had an advance on the novel he was writing. This was very cold.

"Now look you son of a bitch," she said, pointing her finger at Abe. "I want back into that sleazy novel of yours and I want my John back and I want happiness in both of our lives, or you are going to bomb, and you'll shuffle that stack of paper to every publisher in New York and everywhere else with no results, other than another stack of rejection slips." And with this last tirade she walked into the kitchen and ran the faucet for a drink of water.

Abel West walked to the Smith-Corona, turned it on and reached for the stack of paper, drilled it through the platen and down to the last sentence and then calmly typed. "As John Monroe walked out of the alley not even thinking about looking back, he heard screeching tires on wet pavement, a scream and, a muffled thud and then a crash—he turned back when he heard her scream." The kitchen faucet was quiet when he turned off the Smith-Corona.

Abe scribbled on the manuscript to change Monroe's departing one-liner, noting it was lame, and that "get your shit together babe, then give me a call some time." might work better, and then he went into his bedroom and dropped face down into a determined dreamless sleep. Abel West was writing every day.

"Sufficient unto The Day Is the Evil Thereof"

H E'D SLAM BEERS ONE AFTER ANOTHER, not saying a word until he'd finished an even half dozen. It was always after work. He'd come in covered with sawdust and his shirt dark and soaked with his own sweat, then, in for the evening after seeming to relax from that sixth beer it was, he seemed to take in the whole bar. He was a carpenter and began to talk once that initial anesthetic took effect.

He was willing to enter conversation about virtually anything: work, sports, (rarely, but sometimes politics), family life, women, and up to and including quantum physics which I heard him explain once as, "the very, very small and the very, very large and how they are the same thing." He spent almost every evening in the bar. And if he wasn't in the bar, he'd be at home in front of his television drinking strong malt liquor until he passed out. He never missed a day of work and he never missed an evening six-pack and beyond. He also never got out of hand. Though there were a couple times when he carried on until just before closing and had to be carried out after he'd passed out with his forehead on the bar and his arms hanging down akimbo to the floor.

He would drink to relax after eight hours or more of beating a 32-ounce framing hammer into the future homes for the upwardly mobile. He drank to forget about having watched his young wife now years passed on; take five years to die of brain cancer after operations, radiation treatment and painful chemotherapy. He never said an unkind word to anyone unless they became unkind and it was always to their face.

Always ebullient in his drunkenness, he would from time to time, in mid-hoist, take on a faraway smile and hold his glass half full in anonymous skoal, and it would seem as if a force would enter into him that, if uninterrupted, would last a full several minutes with arm cocked and poised half-way between the bar and the wry smile on his mouth.

He'd often listen to other people's problems, nod, emote several kinds deep guttural assertions at each salient point. But he always had the same advice.

"Man, don't ever worry about tomorrow," and he'd look right into their eyes when he said that, then reaching for his beer and looking in the mirror of the back bar, he'd say, "Each day is bad enough." And drain whatever was in his glass and order another one.

Five years after his wife died, he quit drinking, save for one and only one beer at 5:30 every evening after work at the same bar as always. He was standing at the end of the bar the last time I saw him with single beer half-hoist, elbow bent—and a half-smile on face.

In Eritrea While Vietnam Raged

WE WAITED ON HAILE SELASSIE BOULEVARD, deciding where to eat, its namesake having annexed this coastal East African mountain range in the 1950s, after the United Kingdom's soldiers from the British Isles, with the help of the Indian Army, took it away from the Italians during World War II after they had misbehaved by sending their tanks against the cavalry charges of the Ethiopians.

Stationed in Asmara, thirty or so air miles away from Massawa, the Eritrean seaport, where it was 120 degrees or hotter normally, and 98 to 105 in the cool season, we were high in the mountains and back up a long winding road from the sea, where we always had good, cool spring-like weather, which was seldom over 85 or so.

It hardly ever rained in Asmara, and the line of massive palms shaded Italian snooker halls and cafes with espresso machines where I had my first cappuccino in 1969 and marveled at the thick black coffee with cinnamon atop the foamy cream.

Here the Italians had married Eritreans and stayed in East Africa after the war. They called their children *Caffe latte* after coffee and milk. Many still drove old Lancias, and Fiats from the thirties, long after Mussolini stomped around Rome. These cars were sleek short miniatures similar to the Fords and Chevys from the 1930s. I marveled at them driving around in the dusty streets like it was thirty years before.

After a year there, three of us GIs bought a '57 Chevy, abandoning the gharry-cart drivers who whipped their skinny horses, that pulled the rickety carts and our GI asses around the town which the Italians called *Piccolo Roma*. We also toured back roads in Eritrea in our black Bel Air. We once stopped and took pictures of a man leading five camels. We spoke our English talk to him, but he had no idea what nationality we were; we offered our spare change of quarters and half dollars and dimes and he took it in his hand with a puzzled look. When we navigated around his camels, I looked out the back window to see him look at the coins in his hand, then back to the Chevy pulling away, then back to his hand of silver, and then take up the rope to his camels and throw the silver over his shoulder as he began again to walk across the desert. We drove by baboons, and tiny antelope called *dik diks* in acres and acres of cactus and places where an American dollar meant nothing. In Asmara, the Eritrean capital, it was something. We were in the poorest nation on the planet but were soldiers of the richest.

We ate in old world Italian restaurants, on private's wages, where, in at least one of them, tuxedoed Eritrean waiters would serve us seven-course meals, while the cripples begged on the boulevard outside pulling their amputated stumps or useless legs on leather pads with blocks of wood. The seven-course meals were an expensive night out and were only an expedition to be taken after payday, costing us each about seven U.S. dollars.

I probably did no good thing in my eighteen-month tour of duty there, save give beggars and children a little money. The Catholic Church bells, and the Muezzin's call to prayer, rang in the twelve-month springtime air with Coptic Christian priests, who walked the boulevard turbaned, waving black and white monkey-tail swatters at the flies.

At the city's eight-thousand-foot elevation, and at the end of the boulevard at the end of Queen Elizabeth Boulevard, all lined with massive palms, an old Italian man had a restaurant with no waiters. He'd serve you and he spoke no English. He made fish in three separate ways, and perhaps used that many types of fish, and you never knew which one you'd get.

"Ah, *Pesce, Pesce, Pesce!* He would say, finally understanding we wanted fish.

Then we would wait and drink beer, and the fish would come: the meal was always wonderful, with fish from the Red Sea. We were in Eritrea while Vietnam raged, and revolution likewise was in the background here as well. The Eritreans, since 1960, were fighting against the Imperial Ethiopians of Haile Selassie himself. During the brief British rule in the 1940s, some of the folks got a taste of something different than a totalitarian regime.

One day His Imperial Majesty's police had caught a rebel ringleader, performed a quick trial, and in the early afternoon strung him up by quarter-inch steel cable on a hand crank winch attached to a pole and a davit, in a back alley behind the court. Someone down the hall in our barracks witnessed this and described the grisly scene in detail.

That evening, we waited on Haile Selassie Boulevard and argued about which restaurant to go to, and the old man's fish fell into disfavor. We ate at the other end of the Italian-made boulevard that night. While we were dining elsewhere, the Eritrean Liberation Front brought automatic weapons to the old man's café and killed the Judge and the Prosecutor and five customers in several outbursts of gunfire, in revenge for their freshly executed comrade. The next day we who wanted fish, felt strange and lucky. We waited one month before returning to that café which had several new tables, and a freshly plastered wall, but wonderful Italian fish.

The Chef went through the same ritual. "Ah. *Pesce, Pesce, Pesce!*" he said, before disappearing into his kitchen.

It was to be another twenty years before the Eritreans had a nation and changed the names of the streets in Asmara. In the spring of 1970, we were always mindful of home, and mindful that this was not home—while American girls kept writing us letters.

Three Day Pass

WHAT WAS FOR LIONEL HIGHTOWER, the bonus part of his Northern California duty station was that it was only seven hours on the freeway from his home. Home: a grounded splatter of familiar oppression, home with everyone from his high school now locked into a job and kids and mortgage payments, the girlfriend he left when he entered the Army, having married the son of the man who built Disney World in Florida not too long after the dear John letter he received to explain the change of heart in sorrowing detail.

"I wish you well in your Army career," she had written.

His parents and a ten-year younger sibling were a seven-hour drive to visit. But generally, instead of seeing them, several times he ended up drinking with his friend, Monroe Sykes, from High School. Three times that year, Sykes tried to get him to take LSD. Twice he'd declined.

"Yeah why not," Lionel said the third time.

Shortly, Lionel found himself in a grove of tall Douglas Firs. An hour later the continuum of the universe as a part of himself changed how he looked at everything for a drug-induced lapse in mundane time. There was something we were all connected to. He was home—home in the physical sense, having been around the world and culture-shocked several times. He was home in the Oregon that had sent him out like some ancient Greek to find himself at war—or whatever he was supposed to be doing. He hadn't thought about what he was supposed to be doing up until that time. Lionel saw that he had stopped thinking about it for too long of a time. A mile from where he sat was a railway that hauled logs out of the small town twenty miles away through the little farm town where he went to high school. He had hunted deer a mile from this spot. There was wind blowing through the canopy of these Douglas Fir, whistling in a harmonic unison and he believed he saw the stars start to falter, then felt them hit the ground and move and sway and there was a oneness that was all else. He was experienced—just like Jimi Hendrix.

The LSD having dissipated, he drove back to his California base, a long quiet ride down I-5, a cutoff at Willows and down into Santa Rosa, onto 101 to Petaluma, then out toward Dillon Beach and his duty station. He found his company clerk and asked for the 1049 form that was a request to be transferred to the Republic of Vietnam. The company Clerk he'd known for a year assured him he was getting it in, at the right time, as he'd requested this each year and had been denied each time, but now he would go probably in late November, the Company Clerk had said. Lionel took the form that he'd filled out neatly in Government Issue ball point pen and tore it up. They'd had their chance to send him over there. The little piece of paper on Monroe's hand had changed everything. He was experienced—just like Jimi Hendrix. But Hendrix was dead.

Red is Dead

FRED SULLIVAN WAS HIS FOREMAN ON A LARGE TREE PLANTING CREW in Northern California in the early 90s. A mix of hippies and working men, contracted to Big Dog Steve who was a mixture of both, and who planted with the crew, they were planting a large burn that had allegedly been accidently started by pot growers in their nightly clandestine kitchen duties deep in a National Forest. It was 1990 and they had half the contract done; Fred had lost 25 pounds and had a sense of how to get trees to everyone and do the quality control for inspection, as he had planted for six years himself.

It had been going well. They called him Red, but his name was Robert and he was likeably strange, walking on his hands in front of the campfire in the evening where they were all spiked out at camp, and for some reason for a while Fred thought Red had been burying trees. Fred sought to figure this out only to follow him around and find that Red was completely innocent. That would have been stupid since they were being paid by the acre and he was getting an hourly wage, however, trees were being buried. Sometimes Fred would catch guys stashing trees and burning weed in slash piles and taking up the line later after 20-minute breaks, while everyone else slaved in their reforestation Gulag.

After he realized that Red didn't ever do that and understood mostly that he just kept his head down and worked, he respected the guy. Then Red started hanging out with Stomper, a Eugene hippie who blew weed hard every night, and he'd caught Stomper stashing trees red-handed twice.

Red began to get weirder than normal and after the job was over, Fred accidently ran into Red's roommate who told Fred that Red was schizophrenic. The fellow allowed that Red was always OK if he did not go off his medications, but when he did he had a penchant for fire, walking around the house saying, "It's going to burn, it's going to burn, it's going to burn!" Sheepishly Red's roommate admitted that Red, did have a shave in the pen for starting a fire. That, however, was ten years before and the meds were supposed to take care of it.

Later that month Fred was told Red was dead. Fred had heard he and Stomper went on a job in western Idaho and Red who had been off his meds for a month and blowing a lot of weed with Stomper, one day just poured gas over his head, and set himself on fire. Then he, as a burning man, jumped into a holding pond meant to provide water during Forest fires. Red broke his neck in the process of his flaming dive and drowned as the flames were quenched in the pond.

Stomper came back to their camp from town and after smelling a lot of gas and walking around for an hour, he found Red in the pond and had to go back into town and call the State Police who did not exactly figure all this out.

No One Here Gets Out Alive!

IT WAS SUMMER 1970 AND SHE WORKED AT A TOPLESS BAR an hour's drive north of San Francisco. This was a working-class topless bar, in suburban Santa-something in Northern California, with a juke box, red Formica tables, and two dancers who alternated between a footlight-lit platform and pouring golden draughts of beer from chrome-plated pumps. So, she was a country stripper with a good hippie heart and her name was Vivian.

Coins would go in the juke box and eyes, some ogling, would peer through the cigarette smoke and turn toward the dancer. Mounting steps as a low bass thud vibrated the bar, she would in a graceful, but never tacky manner, begin in a way that was like she was entering into water. She'd emerge with a shift of a shoulder and a slight half-round motion of a thigh, the tips of her fingers barely brushing the back of her hips, and she'd begin to dance. Perhaps it is now awkward to write about this electric sensual time. However, the first time I heard "*Oye Como Va,*" by Santana she was dancing.

I remember a small bra with tacky gold lamé tassels reflecting light onto gold wire-framed glasses; auburn red hair spilling long and straight to just above the crack in her ass. The thong was yet to be in vogue, but bikini panties were the dress code. She didn't tease. Laughing, gracefully and joyfully she flashed bright teeth, her head back, breathing deeply, laughing again. I want to remember it in a present tense, like how she plowed perfect arcs in the air with the near perfect peach shape of her ass, as each hip rocked with a beat that is there, stretching out arms behind rhythm (the motion is totally hers). Now, arms move imperceptibly from behind, and in one swift motion breasts neither small nor large began to ride in an undulation with her smile; she had a smile of joy—a smile of joy and rock and roll and yes her breasts were perfect. As I say, I want to remember this. Like remembering the taste of a Camel cigarette just lit off a Zippo lighter even though I stopped smoking in 1990.

I'd been drinking beers fast, it was a half an hour until closing, and to go back and put myself in that place, I'd come here after a late night shift on a military base that I'm supposed to be a part of—in 1970, "back in the day," and if I'm remembering it as present, I'm unwinding, taking it all in and talking to the other dancer, whose name has long since disappeared into remote gray matter, but who I'm interested in—she's pert, conventional, with large breasts that have a few more years, yet they aren't perfect either.

This night Jim Morrison appeals to have his fire lit from the juke. "Come on Baby Light my fire! Try to set the night on fire!" I've secured a breakfast date with this other woman with large breasts, but Vivian, dancing, has everyone's attention, and she is seared into my memory banks from fifty years ago—where I sat ordering beer after beer.

After having returned from an eighteen-month overseas military assignment, I had written off Vivian in that lack-of-confidence way that puts distance wanting, the reality of encounter, and what was then, the days and nights of all-male banter and quip— Vivian, the beautiful Vivian, was the playmate, perfect, an icon, seemingly unobtainable as I'd relegated myself to finding whores in overseas bars but wrote letters to my Catholic bride-to-be on the East Coast. Images coalesce, fade, and become one with juxtaposition, especially when slick magazines sell all the temple goddesses naked and flat on pages while back then affordable whores were procured in the backstreet bars or across oceans in exotic duty in exotic foreign lands. Then thought and desire became an ephemerally concrete touchable presence. The thought of a woman in its essence will sometimes, from sheer loneliness, seem like it will lift the top of your skull off, yet libido is a necessary human attribute as real as your arm or leg.

This night there would be a late-night breakfast and I would gain information that this woman with the huge breasts was living with a real estate agent with a pool and the entire basic high-dollar kept amenities and a seven-year-old somewhere between other scenes, with alcohol or too many barbiturates. The lust would wear off under the glare of neon diner lights and what could have passed for sex with her eventually became unimportant. We went to our separate vehicles.

The summer became hot and there were a lot of late night drives to the beach, and Southern Comfort with its silky sweet medicine glow that helped the waves come in; every few nights after work a number of us would show up and check Vivian out, with the other one with large breasts, quiet, drinking—hardly on the make, yet never giving up either. And then there was this night that their bar and our show had to close for some reason and I was out at another bistro dancing with the pert buxom short topless dancer with all her clothes on and an ample amount of gin, listening to a bad rock and roll band. And in walks a friend of mine with Vivian.

I've a scotch and water to my face, but the way she is walking the length of this bar in a green miniskirt with her hair almost to where her hips are rounding out, there is a lump sticking in back of my throat. She's sitting down now with mouth full of teeth smiling at me, and I know I'm not ever to get more than a hello out of my mouth all evening.

My speech is haltingly glib with one-liners and opulent mannerisms, but the contention is all about the women, loud music, and alcohol. Vivian has not taken her eyes off me, nor mine from her, my friend gesticulating as he gets drinks and pays for them; he asks her if she wants to dance as the band plays something slow. Without looking she says, "Yes, but with him," as she points at me.

Finding touch and movement within arm's reach and looking into incredible eyes framed in gold lenses, blue even in the green of the dance floor, there—what is happening completely by itself makes nothing else cheap or mean any longer; there is a point where the insouciance of lust leaves, focusing simply on the man and the woman of it.

Expectation becomes electrified, meaning reality seems to hold the possibility of being good and warm, our movement together crowds out coincidence and pretense, everybody else seems to take care of themselves and later I kiss her, and what could happen seems not far removed from stars and maybe quantum leaps towards justice as she whispers, *"Tomorrow!"* Tomorrow is always a next day where all goodness is made, and the conversation of the night goes on, floating past our very own existence. That she made this date with me the next day, without offending my friend or hers, seems a bit of art I've not seen before.

That next afternoon I met Vivian at the intersection of two rural Northern California roads. She arrived in a dented and paint-peeling convertible 1953 Austin with a large Great Dane sitting in the front seat with its head sticking over the windshield, its nose straining for an aerodynamic advantage. Without stopping she motioned for me to follow her up this winding California road somewhere close the coast and the small creeks that empty into the Russian River, which, low and green now, had its constant traffic of flocks of summer people. I had met her at the intersection of this small winding road with the more well-traveled highway, and she was leading me away from all this. There had been no word: a bright smile and the Austin spinning its tires and the Dane's unclipped ears that started to flop with the wind whipping them faster as she picked up speed. And Vivian's brownish long red hair flew back in circles, and me in my springy '62 Nova, whining its fourteen-inch tires on the pavement this dry summer day, not exactly sure of where it was going.

But she—after only three or four miles—led me to a brown oak-laden bluff where a ravine ran abruptly under a bridge where there was parking space for two vehicles. We parked, the Dane jumping out immediately, pissing, slobbering, and circling the whole immediate area, smelling me and jumping as high as Vivian's head as she comes over with an open Budweiser in one hand and a joint in the other hand, both of which she hands to me, then puts her arms around my neck and kisses me several times as her breasts push up against the lower part of my chest. This is now beginning to become a reality, and as romance, the heart-pounding uncertainty of passion, had up to that point in my life found not many more concrete places to abide, I am lifted up from the bottom of my feet to some heights I was sure all along had existed. One's own libido has the immediacy of producing high elevation altered states. But I had been a dweller on some flat emotional plateau far too long where there were only rumors of this to be only half-believed, as women and girls seemed to come and go.

There was another woman on a coast far away that I was supposed to marry and, yes, I'd felt this same way about her; there had been romance and sex, but there seemed to be the soap-opera machinations and social trappings that kept you paying out in one way or another just as the whores across several oceans had done for cash, and I was clueless as to which in the grand scope of things was the most honest transaction. The East Coast transaction included the Catholic Church whose honesty was not beyond suspicion. This seemed honest, real, momentary, and abjectly passionate.

Vivian was the original California hip woman in her gold wire-framed glasses, and what she was about to give me in a graceful way, as we started down the ravine with the Dane ahead of us, was totally and completely free. And it was, for a brief time, love. Somehow, I'd missed the Summer of Love when a draft notice showed up. This one afternoon made up for it in a way. We stopped several hundred yards uphill, popped open two aluminum Budweiser cans, and she reached into a bag and took out a quart jar filled with hundreds of charred roaches left over from serious marijuana smoking. She emptied the contents into a rolling paper as she held the jar between her legs, then rolled the paper and its contents deftly into a tight little cylinder and popped it into her mouth, where she lit up with my Zippo lighter, inhaled deeply, her nipples protruding beneath the red t-shirt she wore, and then handed it to me.

The dry crackling heat dissipated in a breeze that came up the ravine; I filled my lungs with smoke and exhaled my whole being as Vivian pulled off her t-shirt. I was, for this moment in time, looking at this topless dancer's breasts as if I were a chaste husband and as if I were the only man in the world who had ever seen them. We sat, talked, and finished our Budweisers. Then she took my hand to lead me a short distance to where an ocher-brown mound of grass protruded from the tan of the dried unshaded green, to lay down a red print cotton cloth in front of a rock outcropping that looked like a clam shell that tried to rise up artfully some long time ago. The dry ground where we lay down seemed to cushion our bodies in a solid way as underneath this August sun we touched, kissed and began to slide hands over one another as sweat began to glisten with the slick human lubricant of making love; the thigh of it, the tongue of it, the tongued nipple of it, the rising up to focus each other's eyes to see and feel the inside of it, the real unseen, only to go down and see and taste the openings of ourselves or the very place where we most completely forget; to leave off the conscious movie of our minds to be, and to have inside us the full emptiness of our being and yes, she smiled and laughed and so did I, and gave into every thrust and pull, backs arched and her body shone with luminescence, with these tanned breasts with nipples to be kissed erect, to leave off and again go down to kiss again the auburn-enshrouded enclosure, intrauterine salt sweet smell and taste, while vaguely seeing her pelvis roll with each touch and taste, and then back to enter, become and then come with her—in her on that hillside under the sun, just as it's been done everywhere always. And then again in its own way it was a single unique irrevocable act as it is to everyone over and over again. We continued to see one another, we became friends, it was never as spectacular as that afternoon. As I said, this was 1970.

There was another topless place in Santa Rosa, "The Marble House," with more supposed class, but it was in reality far seamier, with a dark quality all its own. This was not entirely because it was a topless-bottomless place where customers came for full female nudity. A lighted stage kept a constant line of women taking it off to rock and roll, and then back to the throng of customers to drinks between Elks, Shriners, truck drivers, white college kids, general drunks, all equally perverse and normal at the same time. All the walls were painted black, and the footlights and stage and bar were all presented center front. An upper-level kind of back bar was staged for a more intimate presentation.

Some were on the town some a night away from their wives, some pounding tables, some just sitting there. We were GIs there for the scenery. All patrons were there for the scenery however, with every song on the dance floor, a change in the music as more drinks are poured, different dancers and more banter exchanged, and another female gets the spotlight, as alcohol is passed through a succession of human tubes, in an all-male conflagration of uneasy lust with no immediate outlet other than streetwalkers an hour away in San Francisco (perhaps where more honest transactions could take place); a constant pumping of testosterone from a hundred million inadequacies where the male sexual rite is performed at a tender age as a first act in a bathroom—alone. This is turned into exploitation and the jive commerciality of the erotic so that many never come close to love and sex. Sometimes rock and roll became an antidote to that, sometimes not. The human ocean is not a regulated coming and going of the tides but is often a vast surge only barely restrained (and then only outwardly so) by the fetters of politics, religion, currency, or war.

Back then we were there as GIs and, like all the rest of them, many of our fathers could not explain to us that women were keepers of the next generation and were to be cherished and loved. Even the strippers wanted to be cherished and loved; they were all someone's daughters. No one had explained that to these women either. No one ever told any of us that sex was an appetite to be controlled and used in love. No one told us that we were responsible for our own biology. No one told us that our genome, each unique, was a message in a bottle to be opened up to perhaps reveal something from another world. This, too, was another war being waged.

I went there on a summer night in 1970, with this large-framed Iowa guy, blond with a crag-like face, cratered with the scars from adolescent complexion, complete with blue eyes, which all manifest in a not-unlike-John Wayne manner, an easy and slowly good-humored way that could quite possibly be dangerous as well. He would go to the Oakland processing center to be sent to Vietnam the next day and was not welcoming these travel plans in the least.

The back bar was on a slightly upper level that ran parallel to the stage with a table and was mostly for the daytime business, but was tended at night by a platinum blonde with a less-than-wholesome Lee Remick appearance who, between serving drinks, would dance on a platform attached to the middle of the bar in front of rows of upright bottles of gin and bourbon and the rest of it, all waiting to provide a little comfort and a little death at the same time.

This blonde was the movie star of the place and would always make an impression when she danced and, depending on the music and the tips, sometimes would be better than others. What was there besides sensuality was there only in the way she worked in almost nothing behind the bar with an ability to change into completely nothing in a moment, the way she would turn a cheek while keeping her eyes on you as she would purse her lips while making the change. When she took to the small platform at the center of the bar and took off her bra with quite a bit of show and deep pelvic thrusts rippled her ivory body into curves, and then her ass would tighten and we who had been there before knew eventually she'd unsnap panties and the panties and the skimpy bra would be flung to the back bar and full nudity would float free as she raised her hands in the air; arching back, she would take steps with her long white legs always in perfect time with rock and roll, and then at times in the less-than-bright-light you would see or think you saw something wonderfully pink in the midst of blondness. This male thing of looking at female things has been around since the cave times. It is driven by a sex drive. It is neither profane nor sacred. Neither feminists nor fundamentalists can make it go away. It will always be integral, in the sweet married love beds or dives like this one. It is always there.

There were four bars in the place but where she worked was where the real show was, and where we'd taken my Iowa friend. I'd shared another foreign duty station with him and shared whores in that far-off land, but he now was going to Vietnam where they were really killing us, and we were really killing them. There were no prostitutes in this little Northern California town. This topless-bottomless bar was just like a loaded gun.

So, we sat there drinking, smoking, taking it all in—he's exchanged glances with her, and she has exchanged glances with him, he's liking it; she's at least pretending to like it. I'm a little bored, the music isn't loud enough and it's bad. I've seen all of this. She'd done this to me, so I knew. It was a game she played when the mood was right, and the right person could be involved, and she didn't do it for everyone, but it was always for money, and not everyone would pay. She was a working girl and knew who would pay.

"I'll show it to you for money," was what her wry smile was saying without words. My friend didn't have any idea what was about to come down, as a tall Collins glass, quite empty, is set in front him and he gets blue eyes that match his own full bore in the face that would seemingly swallow him up.

As she takes the platform one more time, the Doors begin to play "Five to One," the bass is thudding and I begin to pay attention again, and by now he probably had enough to remove that heady feeling that yearns to be where the opposite sex is, and the thought for the moment is right on a non-equivocating point of reality, and now she, this very white woman, begins to dance. So here come more deep pelvic thrusts in time with the thudding bass from the speakers. Reflected from the mirror in front of the bar to give your double vision of liquor bottles and full view fore and aft of struts and shakes, plying the smoke-filled bar with her ass as it bends and twists with the music as a small black triangular cloth hides what we assume is a feathery whiteness as blonde as the hair over her shoulders, she unceremoniously takes off a sequined bra which drops at her feet.

I lean over and put a five-dollar bill in the Collins glass in front of my buddy. She almost immediately takes a three-foot stride to step onto the bar in black high heels directly above and peers down upon my friend, who, looking up, catches on and puts another five-spot into the glass. Her thighs are supporting her body now and the gyration of her hips is seeming to orchestrate the music from our point of view, and Morrison bleats "Five to One, Baby, One to Five! No One here gets out Alive!" We'd seen The Doors do this number at Bill Graham's *Winterland* in San Francisco in February prior to this evening. The smoke and the clinking of glasses and hard driving rock and roll permeated the air, my friend puts one more five-dollar bill into the Collins glass, and the music and an incredibly apt torso brings the apex of this twerking triangle closer and closer to his face, which is now becoming a little paler than it normally was. His imagination dissolving in the cigarette smoke as it exhales out his nose and the smoke curls around in blue wisps through the lines in the form of her body, close and approximate to form, a presence not to be known as that night of possibilities rode on for him. She was showing him what he wanted to see. But that night she would never let him do what he wanted to do.

Six months later, he would walk across a compound in South East Asia protected by Marines, who in turn were protected by a battalion of Republic of Vietnam regulars. It was supposedly safe duty, just sweltering heat then six more months and he'd be home for good. He would be walking from a mess hall to an operations building when a Soviet-made rocket launched from twenty-four miles away would blow him fifteen feet in the air, where he'd land in mud and shock, no real pain but that twilight zone of body shock where all is curtailed in bits of noises protracted and clear and memory brings your life in front of you. A mother somewhere in Iowa who held him, several lovers who had held him, a series of dreams and aspirations that had held him, his laughter and humor that had held several of us. Is it sweet precious Jesus who holds him still? Or the pervasive nothingness of before birth, before memory?

It is pervasively sad either way. That night in Vietnam, in shock and unconscious, he writhed eighteen inches away from where he landed and the life that had been with him drained away in the mud and humidity to a dimension that is neither counted by any odds we really know of, whether five-to-one, or one-to-five.

Ring of Fire

"I dreamed we were doing "Ring of Fire" with Mexican Trumpets!"
—*Johnny Cash*

CHARLIE AXELROD WAS IN THE RED SEA, diving down and coming up for air; then down again, and he went down once more swimming along the red coral reef. He emerged to snorkel on top to see what he could see directly below. Five miles north of Massawa, Eritrea that January in 1970, yellow and striped Blue Butterfly fish, Clownfish, Dottybacks, all teemed that day in bathtub-warm aqua-blue marine water.

That morning thirty GI's had an African beach to themselves, with iced-down beer in five twenty-gallon shining galvanized trash cans. All in two U.S. Army deuce-and-a-half's and their shift at operations had four days off. Charlie got to this strange place somehow by volunteering for Vietnam in 1968 and found himself instead in Africa, and this reef was the most amazing thing an Oregon farm boy had ever seen, apart from baboons that threw rocks and mostly missed. But this alive swimming Technicolor water, with waving fans of red, white and light-yellow coral and the turquoise blue patch reef was on the other side of a sand plain. As he swam, the reef gave way and dropped off to a dark blue to become a fringe reef, and the fish were bigger.

The reef humped over more, and he continued going down the reef where the water was a little deeper and then dropped down into darkness. Then when he came to the comfort of the reef, on the edge, Charlie saw it to his right—and he saw it full on, tip-to-tail, then, with an autonomic explosion, his body had him over the top of the reef, swim fins moving like instinct moves things fast; his mind did not say "Shark!" much less perceive "Tiger shark, approaching 20 feet," but it was the biggest damn thing he'd ever seen big enough eat him coming out of darkness. Over the top of the reef the sand plain turned to chest-deep water after about thirty feet and he had his fins off and was running back to the beach.

Charlie remembered his friend 100 feet away and could see his snorkel and started yelling, and when his friend's head came up and he heard "Shark!" as Charlie yelled, he saw a replay of his own frantic exit. Breathlessly they made it back to the beach. After a half-mile walk back, they found that the First Sergeant had drunkenly driven the deuce-and-a-half into a sea grass meadow and got it stuck on the African beach at low tide. When they got there the First Sergeant was drunkenly digging out their transport home and they wisely grabbed beers and went up the beach.

About a quarter mile away from their GI binge there was an Italian film company making a movie about a boy in a raft, and they had cameras rolling and were shouting in Italian from a bullhorn in a larger boat and had fake shark fins on floats in the water around the boy in the raft. They looked closely at Italian actresses in bikinis swimming with man-eaters and drank their beer, ignorant of their short distance from the reality that mimicked their enactment. Charlie and his companion shook their heads at the irony of it, but they knew no Italian (and the Italians wouldn't talk to them anyway) and the irony wafted away over the shimmering blue-water heat.

While the cameras rolled that morning—others in their outfit were in Phu Bai taking North Vietnamese rockets, with many of them getting addicted to heroin, while Charlie and his comrades drunkenly kept East Africa that year, none of them knew that 120 miles to the south of the beach *Bab-el-Mandeb* was the land bridge that had enabled humanity's walk out of Africa when ice-age waters receded and oceans and man were purposed to begin the long walk from an Eden to the ends of the earth.

Twelve years later Charlie heard Mexican trumpets belting it out during Semana Santa in Lo de Marco, after he'd returned from the jungle where parakeets and jaguars had their homes, and before Charlie took his evening ramble down the beach he thought of this African beach, and the meal Charlie might have become, and how since then, sometimes softer but no less dangerous things have come out of darkness. That day in Mexico   pelicans flew in formations above the beach palapa that sold beer and you could see the three islands of Tres Marias in the setting sun, and this world aflame landed close peril at his doorstep from the magnanimity of a shark attack to car wrecks and near miss happenstance, dangerous girlfriends and a mugging leaving a knife scar. He had lived in the midst of blessings and beauty and they were continuing to appear. Thinking of all of these experiences came to him thirty years later— once he'd been heralded by Mexican trumpets. Even before *Bab-el-Mandeb* these long walks had been good.

Smitty Smith Heads Home

SO, YOU MUST IMAGINE THAT SMITTY'S BLUES were all pervasive. You must dust off your copy of Miles Davis' "Sketches of Spain," pull out the vinyl, from its album cover and sleeve and know there was something else about to happen. If you've never waited in anticipation for a needle to hit the grooves of a vinyl record with a slight static pop and with an anticipation of hearing something glorious, then you have no idea what I'm talking about.

That afternoon I couldn't talk him out of playing his saxophone in his barracks cubicle for an evening in San Francisco with pals. Smitty didn't like to leave base much unless it was a jazz bill somewhere, or a concert worth catching at the Fillmore. Plain carnality was not Smitty's style. An evening in the Enlisted Men's Club was most every evening's entertainment for him. Records, LPs, albums new and old, old blues men, Jimi Hendrix, Dizzy Gillespie, comedy, Moms Mabley, Redd Foxx all were a wall of safety and solitude. Stereophonic proclamations inside his cubicle in an eight-man bay, with two other blacks' both musicians, whose horns would blare with Smitty's and echo down the hall live, or the needle would drop down to the vinyl and you'd hear Miles, or somebody else behind the door, or if the doors and windows were open the melody would echo from the hall to a good portion of the small army post.

The integrated Army was mostly white; the black men inside it was mostly controlled by white men. There, however, something else going on. Smitty much like myself had about five months left on his enlistment and Vietnam was over with for him. Smitty would go home, play music, it was a waiting game. Smitty would go home.

Smitty was a bluesman. Hip. Got it. Affable. He walked with a swaggering sway that was poetry and when he put his saxophone to his lips the nondescript concrete government building, despite its drabness, could become harmony for a second or two, or thirty second melody, a trill, a riff, a combination a chord, or disjunction. Then sometimes he and the others would jam. Without sound, the OD green army drab pervaded. With it, drabness went away in our minds perhaps even for a second or two.

When it came back, relief from boredom off duty was only three hundred yards away at the Enlisted Men's Club. Smitty sits in the EM club with gin and tonics—an extensive line of gin and tonic—himself and the TV, Johnny Carson, after contrails of the war with the 10 o'clock news. There was the bartender, and himself.

A black sergeant in starched fatigues, who is Charge of Quarters, makes his rounds around the base and makes his stop in the bar in the enlisted man's Club. As I said Smitty was a bluesman. hip, got it, affable, there was poetry every time he opened his eyes.

"What kind of rice you eat, Smitty?" asks the CQ.

"It ain't Uncle Ben's!" says Smitty.

"What kind of pancake syrup you eat Smitty?" asks the CQ.

"It ain't Aunt Jemima's, Homes!" says Smitty laughing.

"And hot breakfast cereal?" asked the CQ, leaning forward ominously with military precision toward Smitty's bar stool.

"It ain't Cream O' Wheat!" says Smitty.

You would have to remember the Cream of Wheat cereal box with the black servant wearing the chef's hat on the front with the seemingly beckoning wholesome goodness coming from the pictured bowl of grits. The Aunt Jemima's bottle, and the Uncle Ben's box did the same job of offensive embodiment of racist stereotype with the goodness of food in the land of good and plenty, but in a society organized of want, poverty and overt racism. Now why I must explain this recedes in a rearview mirror, then comes back as billboard in the headlights because it's not gone away.

"Black!" says the CQ, nodding his head.

"Black!" says Smitty, as no one in the bar gets the antidote to iconic racist advertising images flying out of reality as rage is supplanted by humor.

The CQ makes a crisp about-face with his clipboard, and heads out into the lobby, out the door and into the night. Smitty's salute was the wave of his Gin and Tonic the split second before the CQ began his about-face.

More gin and tonics: Smitty thought of the back streets of Oakland being different than the back streets of Baltimore where he's from. There was war in both cities in 1970. Smitty knew Baltimore, but not Oakland. Sonoma County, California was neither.

Smitty didn't frequent local bars, because they were too white, or maybe they were too lame, or maybe both in this egg-and-butter country that is Northern California where he was aware that the reality was that it could warp and be Mississippi. More gin and tonics, in a safe enlisted man's club in an out-of-the-way American Army base in rural Northern California. This was as I say 1970, no one ever imagined the population would double here, with a blanket of houses all the way to the Golden Gate—fifty miles away.

This bar, like all specifically government architecture, is designed to give no surprises, to let the human mind be led unthinking down chartreuse and puke-green corridors without the remotest possibility of a truly original thought taking place, or anything else dangerous to the scheme of things. Same bricks, same floor plans worldwide. Government planned. Our enemies the Soviets did the same thing.

This particular enlisted men's club, once you step out of upholstered seats of the bar, is that exact sameness—the same smell of floor wax, the exact same latrine, where Smitty is taking his clothes off, thinking he's in the barracks because, well, because of too many gin and tonics, he's taking his clothes off and about to walk down the hall to his room, taking his clothes off in the latrine as he always does when he's drunk. He's drunk, but he's still in the EM club bathroom that is exactly like his barracks bathroom, as I said.

It was late and he's careful so as not to wake up roommates with short tempers, taking clothes off and thinking he's about to make it to his room, where a four-by-six poster of Angela Davis greets all who enter. All the white NCOs have not been able to figure out how to make him take the poster down. And now he's walking down the hall naked with fatigues in one hand, boots in the other, down this hallway which looks "just like," but is not, the barracks three hundred yards away. But it *is* the hallway leading to Temporary Dependent housing, where Non-Commissioned Officers' families get to stay until there is housing available in the on-base tract homes.

Smitty now walking naked down the hallway to what he was sure was his room, the crossing-the-street-part that he did every previous night had melded into his consciousness and having been in the men's room outside the EM club which is you will remember exactly, architecturally alike in all respects, he had taken his clothes off there and as he headed for the door, he finds it unfamiliarly locked—the barracks doors were never locked. Smitty stands in front of the locked door and begins to bang on it with Joe Frazier-sized fists, and Smitty is getting really pissed.

"Open up, Homes, open up. Hey, homeboys, hey Muthafukahs! It's me MUTHAFUKAHS!" Smitty yelled.

His voice got louder and echoed down the hall. A bleached-blonde in curlers, fresh in from some other assignment of her Master-sergeant husband, opened the door. She didn't stop screaming until the MPs arrive, with Smitty still standing there in the hall, his fatigues in one hand, boots in the other, all of him swaying back and forth, naked Smitty weaving back and forth, eyes half open in a night void of explanation.

The next morning Smitty's roommate was explaining all of this to Smitty sitting on his bunk and Aretha Franklin is somehow diminutively coming out of his stereo through the headphones lying on his bunk. "I heard it through the grapevine, not much longer would you be mine." Aretha sings.

Smitty's roommate tells him there is an appointment to explain all this to the Commanding Officer at noon. It is 11 am and Smitty rubbing his head is disbelieving.

Six months after that we were in Ft. Hood, Texas. It was summer—humid, several thousand acres of military base, acres and acres of tanks, armored personnel carriers, almost everybody in a sea of olive drab, a lot of officers, a lot of shit to take or dodge or hide from, and helicopters whirling overhead, over barracks with mostly male humans that are supposed to have the ability and verve to climb into these large hunks of mechanized metal, drive them onto huge jet airplanes, to be taken any place at all in the world and, well, take over on a few moments' notice, and, as an Army does, shoot the people that needed shooting.

From time to time our nation really needed to do that, and as far as any of us knew we would really need to do it again. That it didn't really work that way seemed to be beside the point. But that was the pretense at least. So, there was the heat, a relatively rolling landscape coupled with an outside-the-main gate Army town that was void of a community save for gas stations, pawnshops, whorehouses and the prejudices of race and color mostly, where the lack of the local dialect could get you in trouble too, if you couldn't squirt out a "Y'all" at the precise moment or if you happened to be black. All in all, it was a hatred symbiotic to the overt evil of the adjacent institution in which we labored in our green fatigues as the worker bees, but our military-industrial economy supplied the town with commerce. This all came in concert to make it an institution populated by 50,000 inhabitants, the large majority of whom were from somewhere else—including many recent visitors to Vietnam— a place where perhaps our Army should never have been.

There was an incident that started out innocent on the 4th of July and shooting Roman candles at each other which then became a full-on race riot when the MPs showed up. Some were desperate men with $100-a-day heroin habits brought back from Vietnam with the necessity of buying Mexican Brown heroin in the outskirts of the humid little Army town. Two MPs were found in a dipsy dumpster when things went wrong after the Fourth of July shootout with Roman candles, when they were sent in to quell the frivolity and were simply outgunned. But this was Texas, with the stink of dead armadillos on the back roads, and an enlisted men's club the size of two football fields where usually once a month somebody got shot or knifed, often over somebody else's wife. There were hushed-up race riots with an over-proportioned number of African-Americans, as the Army had created its own ghetto of inhabitants taught to hate in an efficiently remorseless manner by going to other countries to kill folks different from ourselves, not realizing everyone is different from ourselves and with the mistaken notion that we all own our own souls, and if we do unto others by doing what we are told that is somehow always right—even though this was antithetical to the original proclamation.

There was strangeness along with a colloquial geography, a political strangeness, that had kept the 20th Century from dealing with harmony—perhaps because it was the bloodiest century in human existence. But all of this, by the time I got there, was about over for me, just like this story is about over. In two more months, I was to be a civilian. I figured this was the worst place I'd ever been, and it was about par for the Army to release me here.

I was married now and that was just fine. I'd made sergeant and she was a nurse and we were just fine. The Army, though, is about the guy that is next to you and that guy might be a hundred guys before it is over with. I was married and therefore free from the barracks life, but I was not free from those I'd been next to. And I had a rucksack I kept at home ready to load through on a C-141 cargo jet to anywhere they wanted to send us, and we maneuvered with infantry and armored units to be ready for the sending.

Austin was only a couple hours away. My wife had taken a trip to the East Coast to see her mother and I had just come back from Austin after having procured some fresh LSD just in from California, and I was walking in these barracks where Smitty, who had been sent here also, was lying on his bunk in shorts, and I walked over to him just as the tone arm on his stereo laid into the groove of Hendrix/Dylan's "All Along the Watch Tower" from the speakers above on his wall. It was 7 p.m. and very humid. I walked up to Smitty's bunk. I place a small piece of purple paper next to his hand, one like I had ingested thirty minutes before. He's never had this stuff before and has always maintained that he never would. I had said that too—once. You must remember this was 1971 and it was technically still in the decade of the sixties.

"Say what?" Smitty says. His eyes light up and he tilts his head and rolls his eyes.

"Acid," I say.

Smitty rolls eyes at me and then back to the purple piece of paper, and without another word puts it in his mouth. Forty-five minutes later the chartreuse and puke green of the military base walls were aglow, and we were both doing a lot of laughing. By the time we make it outside, it is just past sunset and mercury vapor lights have torched the rows of wooden barracks a dark purple hue. We walk down streets with graveled shoulders that bead together and start to form patterns that vibrate. Somehow the energy of Creation itself was starting to rush up from my diaphragm, under my solar plexus and out my palms. Smitty is shaking his head back and forth and walking.

"I don't fucking believe this!" he said.

We leave for a walk that took us through the rows and rows of barracks, fenced-off motor pools and acres of military might, through company streets where we were not known, and back again toward our company of GIs, with our particular expertise in a global defense effort by the United States.

The landscape congeals and gives off amber green hues; it was darker, and the first stars are starting to appear. The ground and pavement ripple in fractal resonance, there are non-drug-induced tarantulas crawling through the nighttime—as there were always tarantulas crawling through the nighttime. There is a moving and we both seem to have a clue that we're a part of this moving movement that has no politics. Somehow in this state we tapped into pure joy despite our hapless assignment.

We found our way back to the barracks and an outdoor basketball court. Smitty slam- dunked an imaginary basketball, I took the same basketball out, passed off to Smitty, who made a short jump shot with this ball of ours that never misses. I take it out again, and it's one-on-one for a while then into the boards for lay ups, back out, and it went on for a good half an hour until I collapse on the ground, laughing, laughing for what seemed another half an hour. We were still laughing—I'm sitting on a hydrant now and Smitty standing, as an Afro-American soldier in starch crisp OD green fatigues of the U.S. Army, walking out of the night, at his own cadence, his spit-shined black jump boots reflecting light from the mercury vapor inside and above us and grabbing with each step on the thin gravel with a distinct rhythm echoing down the company street.

"Say Black," a deep guttural voice says.

"Say Black," Smitty answers as he passed, and they exchange a salutary five dap, as he walks back into the night. I knew Smitty did not know this soldier.

"Jesus man," I say lamely to Smitty, while still laughing through this altered state.

"You know, I wish I could do that." I say rather lamely.

"YOU, muthafucker," Smitty says, laughing the same laugh that started an hour before and pointing at me.

"YOU, muthafucker… CAN'T!"

We laugh in the bright luminescence of this timeless night with tarantulas crawling across the pavement and merciless mercury vapor lights lighting up acres of barracks and acres of tanks, and as we laughed we were longing for the blue breaking-up-dawn that was hungering for an end to war: an end to war in foreign lands, and an end to the war in ourselves.

Earned Wisdom

I HADN'T BEEN HOME LONG ENOUGH TO TAKE A SHOWER and there came a pounding on the door, and I knew only too well who it was, and he was the last person in the world I wanted to see. I answered the door.

"Ah, Heartache, my old friend," I said, "come in, you son of a bitch, come on in and make yourself at home. You know your way around. There's beer in the refrigerator. I gotta grab a shower."

He didn't say a word, but he headed for the Hotpoint refrigerator next to the Frigidaire gas stove. I got in the shower and washed off the grime from the roofing job I'd hated for the last month.

One more week and that would be done. Then, hopefully, the rains would start. I'd be off with unemployment checks until an editing job promised to me turned up in January. In the meantime, I could get some of my own writing done without worrying about the wolves at the door.

This guy and his friends, however, were worse than wolves. I got out of the shower, dried off, wrapped a towel around my waist, walked through the bathroom door, and there he was, with his feet propped on my coffee table watching the six o'clock news. He had gone through one sixteen-ouncer. He annoyingly belched and then gargled with the last bit of the first beer as he was opening the second one. I'd been expecting him, but I had hoped he'd gone back to California where he belonged.

"Looking kind of down in the mouth," I said.

"Been with that bitch Self-Pity again, haven't you?" I said.

"You sick bastard, we all know how she treats you!" I said.

I went back to my bedroom. I finished drying my hair and put on some shorts and an old Hawaiian shirt. Then I hit the fridge and zipped open a tall boy for myself. I just sat there, eyeing the tube with as much attention and chagrin at the commercials as

Heartache gave David Muir. I wanted him out of the apartment but felt a strange premonition that he needed to be there. Then there came another knocking at the door. I answered and there he stood: Misery, in Friday night togs, looking like an escapee from a disco pogrom from decades ago.

"Yeah, I might have known it would be you," I said as I opened the door.

"Come in; it seems I've got some company you're gonna love. The beers are where they stay cold."

It wasn't three minutes before there I was, with both of them on my couch, drinking my beer. After a round like this two months ago, I'd gotten into a card game, then behind on the cable bill, and there would be no football until I went back to work in January.

I brought out a can of oily sardines and a bag of chips before they got around to yelling for food. I'd scarcely gotten the hosting job done when a banging started at the back door.
"Who the hell could this be now?" I said out loud.

I made my way back through the rubble of beer cans on the back porch with its idle fishing poles and the washing machine that never worked, and there he was—his left shoulder facing me, looking up into the sky at the bright, almost neon, October twilight with its changing colors that were solemnly turning gray—and there he was.

"Loneliness, you bastard," I grumbled. "At least you brought beer." I made my way back into the apartment, Loneliness shuffling in behind me.

"Look who's here, boys," I yelled.

I went for another one of my beers. I knew Loneliness brought the cheapest beer money can buy, but at least he brought some. Every three months, with the change of the seasons, it seemed he abandoned whatever twelve-step he was in and ended back on my back porch with the cheap beer. I made my way into the living room. They all were making a lot of noise without saying anything. Now Heartache was whining about Self-Pity and whether she was going make it back into town.

"That's all I need," I said out loud, "is to have her show up tonight."

I made a mental note not to let her in if she did. When I discovered that there was nowhere to sit, I took to the floor in front of the tube. They'd switched on a two-month-old golf tournament where a football game should have been, so I knew it was going to be a bad night. Then I heard the door begin to bang. I didn't move, but it got louder and louder. I let it bang, and they all began to grumble.

"Go away, you bitch!" I yelled.

"Answer the damn door!" said Loneliness.

Heartache got up expectantly to answer the door, thinking it might be her. He'd been dating her for three years; each time it would last a couple weeks to a month, then she'd jilt him again, and here he would be.

"SIT YOUR ASS DOWN! We don't have enough beer. The last time all four of us were together, she came in a mini-skirt all hiked-up with torn-ass nylons, and she brought whiskey, and her nice tits, and the two of you got in a fist fight and tore this place to pieces after only about thirty minutes."

Loneliness thought he heard a woman's voice from the front porch. "Let me in!" Self-Pity cried.

"GO AWAY!" I screamed. "If I let you in, all your troubles will come, too! Get off my damn doorstep!"

"She'll go away eventually," I said as I turned my back on the door.

I got back to the golf tournament. There were eighteen beers left in the fridge. I began to drink peacefully in my empty room.

And How

"I CAN'T TAKE THIS ANYMORE," she yelled, suddenly. "You're staying out until one or two in the morning, coming home drunk, tipping over furniture, and last week putting your foot through the TV that I'd left on just so I wouldn't feel so goddamn lonely.

"The swearing and ranting you do, with no good reason, other than you're pissing drunk. Then your damn hangovers, night-of-the-living-dead hangovers, wanting-to-sleep-all-day hangovers.

"And when you do finally come to, eating the entire contents of the refrigerator at one sitting, and now you're up for your second drunk driving ticket and will probably do ten days in jail, lose your damn license for a year.

"And I'll have to drive your sorry ass everywhere you want to go and that won't be enough because you'll be yelling at me about how I drive.

"And your fucking poetry, big-deal poetry, half-ass, two-bit poetry that-has-never-paid-the-rent-poetry—oh well yes, once when that Canadian company paid you $250 for the entire press run of your book.

"And all your damn friends that are poets, the half of whom, you tell me you mildly loathe after they leave, having drank all of our beer, because they have drunk all of our beer.

"At least two of them have jobs teaching it in junior colleges. But not you, you wouldn't be caught dead teaching a creative writing class. A man of the street you call yourself—Jesus, if it wasn't for me, you'd be out on the street as a homeless person.

"And in three months you'd be mumbling and having the DTs again, and goddamn it, at least three times in the past month, you've come home wanting to make love, then can't because you're too drunk to fuck and pass out..."

The finger pointing stopped and I realized as I sat up in bed that this woman and I had been divorced fifteen years, she was remarried with children that were not my own, and how she lived on the opposite side of the continent from me, and how it wasn't *that* bad, and how I'd never hear this, and how I'd probably have to watch it for a while.

We All Called Him Pappy

H E WAS A SURLY, WHISKER-BRISTLED UN-ROY ROGERS-like, half-Blackfoot Indian, cowboy, who daily poured himself out of last night's bottle of fortified wine and into a squinched up grease stained Stetson that mostly never came off the top of his head. He rolled his own cigarettes and chain-smoked Top tobacco out of a can from the moment his eyes opened in the morning until they closed the next evening. He had an almost Jack Elam right eye and rode a horse he called Jean Autry—well he had another name for the horse but if I write it down this will never be printed.

We all called him Pappy. There was a rumor, which I always discounted, that his name really was Frank Gray. For a time, Pappy, twice to three times a week, would ride his horse to the bar and tie Jean Autry to a light pole between a row of cars and come in to drink the cheapest draft beer in the county—we were all there to drink the cheapest draft beer in the county.

Often, we collectively encouraged him when he was in an inebriated state, because we were all generally in an inebriated state, to ride his horse around the pool table in the bar where everyone knew everyone else's face even if we could rarely remember each other's names. Some of us generally had forgotten our father's name in the state we were in. That seemed to happen once a week, for about a year until the owners spent several grand on a new hardwood floor—and Jean Autry and her horseshoes were no longer welcome.

Pappy was good at drinking Diamond Red wine, poaching deer, and breaking horses. He was generally bad at gold mining, smoking pot, and women. Pappy lived out of his saddle and sometimes under bridges and lots of times on the edge of deep timber with his horse and a campfire, at times with anyone who would put up with him. He was a Korean War Veteran and claimed to have been shot up, stomped on, broke legged shit-on throughout most of his life and had the scars to prove it.

There was a six-month spread when Pappy had a seventeen-year-old girlfriend who ran away from an affluent but oppressively violent home 200 miles away, and somehow hooked up with Pappy, bought herself a Welsh mare, and rode everywhere Pappy did. With a floppy hat and a Rubenesque figure, she put Pappy through his paces and had him riding with the wind boiling through his horse's mane. She had been the slightly chubby rich girl from grade school whose father bought her and her sisters fine Arabian geldings. She knew during this pleasant upbringing, nothing of what she learned underneath the starry, starry skies with her very own cowboy horse-trainer Blackfoot Indian who fed her stories on the 17th parallel and showed her the finer points of horse sense. She'd take the six months with Pappy with her all her life, but six months was probably enough. Her mare's name was Pinkie.

Pappy taught her everything he knew about horses, which was considerable. Pappy never got on a green unbroken horse, but through a myriad of rope tricks would take the wildest mustangs and with the knowledge of their pressure points have them behaving like tame well-trained dogs in a matter of a just a few days sometimes. They'd walk around the corral with their ear at Pappy's shoulder.
"Stop!" he'd holler. And the horse would stop.
"Back!" he'd holler. And the horse would begin to back up. Then around the corral they'd go again. Then sometime after that was standard, Pappy would put a saddle on the horse. After the same drill with the saddle, Pappy would get on the horse and ride. This generally took about a week or less.

Jean Autry and Pappy and his girlfriend and Pinkie had come off the Dead Indian highway after a trip up to Lake of the Woods in the early fall camping, eating poached deer and living in the crisp night air by a campfire bundled up in a zip-together sleeping bag bedroll.

Sadly, a log truck spooked Pinkie and she threw her young equestrian into the ditch, but Pinkie got clipped hard by the back tires of the truck that swayed out onto the shoulder of the road. Pappy had to shoot Pinkie, and had a friend come get the dead horse and haul it to his ranch, where Pappy butchered up Pinkie and passed some of the steaks around. This didn't sit well with his seventeen-year-old girlfriend and after that she dumped him and went home to her parents. Pappy went on the skids for a short while after that.

On one of those bad nights after his heaven-sent young woman rode away into the sunset, several of us watched him stagger out of the bar, too drunk to climb on his horse, and we were too drunk to help him without being kicked. After several attempts to swing an uncooperative leg over the saddle, Jean Autry finally got her head down between Pappy's legs and lifted him front ways over her neck and got Pappy into the saddle, facing backwards, but nonetheless mounted on his steed; Pappy eventually got turned around and then Jean Autry walked through the streets and back to their camp under the bridge while Pappy slept in his saddle.

Pappy convinced anyone he met that he couldn't read. Yet the fact was that he had consumed all of Steinbeck, Hemingway, Zane Gray and of course Louie Lamour, but he'd not dream of letting anyone know he was literate.

"It's detrimental to your health to let anyone know you know anything." he said.

He was charming for about ten minutes and could get any woman's attention for at least that long, but the long bouts with Diamond Red and sleeping under bridges made that about the limit of duration for all but the most curious.

"Katy bar the gate! There's a Recess in Heaven! For an angel, has entered our midst!" he'd say perched at the front bar stool as a woman would enter the bar. And he was perennially on the first stool by the entrance. He seemed always to be ready for arcane adventure toward easy money of some kind and would stop at nothing this side of armed robbery. There were hundreds of failed, but at the time surefire gold schemes, all ending up with him as broke as he began and pockets as empty as the bottles of Diamond Red strewn around his camp.

Pappy had a problem with a bad tooth on a cold winter's evening and tried to get some clinic or welfare agency to help him out of his agony. After three days of no luck he took a twenty-pound rock and put it through the glass door of the police station. When a beehive of cops appeared and he was arrested, he made them take care of his bad tooth. He did seventy-two hours in the can and was out with his dental problems behind him.

He disappeared for several years into the Siskiyou mountains, the border between Southern Oregon and Northern California, with a string of horses and a giant woman and a gleam in his eye, and with stories about sure gold strikes.

Some years later was the last time I saw Pappy. I had first run into him in the same bar ten winters before I sat there talking to him for the last time. He'd just been released from a California penitentiary after he'd had his third heart attack there. He had gone to the pen because he'd given up his gold, for growing pot in the remote roadless areas he'd not been able to strike it rich on. He'd apparently had some serious success with this enterprise and paid cash for a five-acre parcel close to a National Forest and a shack and a barn and good corral for horses and he was with the same woman he left town with. He'd begun however, to have heart problems and only jail had stopped him from drinking and smoking.

When some redneck thought the skinny cowboy with heart problems could be taken advantage of and reneged on paying for a couple pounds of hand-grown pot, Pappy beat a man twice his size almost to death with a two-by-six.

He was wide eyed, albeit a little pale looking, and drinking draft beer with the same giant woman I'd seen him disappear with years ago.

"I've had six heart attacks!" he said, greeting me with a wild-eyed grin.

"The last three was in the state pen." He was pulling on his beer like a man who'd just walked across the Mojave Desert. His old perilous grin and a different appearance somehow, perhaps serenity, perhaps enlightenment, perhaps he was just damn glad for being out of jail. But after the brief greeting and small talk he turned to me like an evangelist.

"Now don't you ever be afraid of dyin'. The last heart attack I just plum crossed over to the other side and saw me a rainbow bigger than this whole damn valley! I saw great streams of colorful lights, the likes you've never seen, I seen green like you never seen; ah there's horses there too! And there was peace like I've never felt, all so beautiful makes me want to bawl like a baby just thinking it. I saw my little brother there, the one that had died back on the Res. A feeling I had that is the happiest feeling this sorry son-of-a-bitch has ever felt. No worry, no guilt, no pain, no wanting anything. Then I woke up with this pencil-necked intern pulling a big horse needle out of my chest."

"You son-of-a-bitch!" I said. 'Why the hell did you do that? I don't need back in this forsaken hell-hole of a place, goddamn you, goddamn you!" I said.

"The skinny little bastard looked like; he'd seen a ghost, he did!" Pappy laughed and was drinking out of a large pitcher by now.

"That was three weeks ago. They told me I couldn't drink, or smoke again," he said, lighting a tailor-made Pall Mall off the one he'd just had in his mouth.

"They let me out of jail because they said I'd die before I'd serve out the next three years of my sentence," Pappy said.

As he began surveying around the bar as if someone was listening that should not get this information, he was wide-eyed and almost contrite. I'd not really seen him this way ever. He got out of jail and his woman just drove him north across the Oregon-California border because she now lived back in Oregon, having sold their place and horses and everything with Pappy being in jail.

"Don't ever be afraid of dyin' ever!" he coughed, wide-eyed and as seriously adamant as I'd ever seen him.

"If a son-of-a-bitch like me has got that to look forward to, you're all going to be just fine!" he said motioning a benediction up and down the bar. The smoke was wafting up toward the ceiling fans; Universalism, and the rumble of beer glasses, music, and a mumble of the rest of the barflies prevailed. I'm pretty sure I was the only one who heard this story that night.

The Fire Itself

THAT THIRD SUMMER AFTER THE HULL MOUNTAIN FIRE, Leonard Moore picked black-cap raspberries with his youngest son where the upper cabin had been. They made pie that day with their booty, a half dozen pies, with the sweetest of wild tart taste baked in their propane oven late in August with the doors open in their small cabin. If you had been there, you'd have gotten a slice, as they shared them with friends, and perhaps the pies were a rite of passage. Len had survived two years of divorce and single fatherhood, raising a boy from three years old pretty much by himself.

He now had become adept at answering all questions from a five-year-old with perhaps not all the facts. That day they were picking berries amid purple fireweed which, like the raspberries, were growing in profusion after the fire, healing the fire-scarred earth and blowing white seed across the steep hill, in a lightly purpled white breeze.

They were at the site of the upper cabin that had been destroyed in the fire. That landscape, still black where the fire had burned and where the black-cap raspberries had vined into profusion, was now delivering black goodness one-by-one into his stainless-steel pail five feet from where the steps had been—and his son was happy. Two years before this afternoon he'd put his cherubic three-year-old face into his small hands and watered them with tears. "I have lost my family!" little Robinson sobbed.

However, one year before that miserable day, Len had tended the fire line he built with his oldest son Charles before the fire hit their place. With a shovel and Pulaski, he and the thirteen-year-old lad constructed a five-inch-wide crease in the forest floor exposing unburnable mineral soil as serviceable as asbestos. After exploding into a 100-acre blow torch in the box canyon over the ridge, the fire spilled slowly downhill, creeping and calming to an eventual wall of flame, scarcely a half mile from the ridge and thirty feet from their back door; then holding there at their shovel-and-Pulaski-built line, the mineral soil stopping its hot creep.

It was determined that the fire was started by an arsonist. It started about two miles from Len's home, raged to several hundred acres and started down Ramsey Canyon west and to the north of their home. The first evening with none of this news, other than the very visible column of smoke, Leonard hiked to the ridge to take it in with a little more than trepidation. He did not know which direction it was heading and did not know what he would find. The smoke walking up the ridge was out in the distance it seemed, walling up billows that he could see up and through the Douglas fir, cedar, ponderosa pine and madrone forest. He had been to a Forest Service fire school three years before and had been on several small wildfires. What he did know from the education the federal government provided, was how anything related to wildfire in the Pacific Northwest could go seriously wrong and did so on a regular basis.

On his desk lay a book by Norman Maclean he'd just finished called *Young Men and Fire*, an account of the Mann Gulch fire in Montana where fourteen fire fighters lost their lives. Two weeks before the fire he was looking at, the Storm King Fire in Colorado killed fourteen fire fighters from the Prineville Hotshots. Leonard had worked with one of them, a biologist, a thoughtful and dedicated woman, who joined the agency's fire suppression effort in addition to her duties as a biologist. Each of these incidents involved a fire crew being overrun by a raging wildfire, and each was an instance of being in the wrong place at the wrong time. In addition, each was an incident of poor decisions by management that sent bright young folks to their deaths in a maw of hell.

Mounting the ridge and a little out of breath, Leonard saw the northward flowing blanket of billowing motion ahead of Neil Rock and the cliff. He walked up to the abutment of the big outcropping of limestone and was climbing up the top to its small plateau, to make his way to the north side for a better view, as there was a timber and manzanita patch between himself and a panorama of the fire. To his left below there was a box canyon, the classic box canyon taught in fire school as a fatal trap that will rapidly burn just like fire in a full-on roaring furnace.

"Len!" he heard someone call his name. It was Kent, one of his neighbors. They didn't speak until Kent caught up.

The northward flowing blanket of billowing smoke he'd seen before the north edge of Neil Rock was a fire of about six or seven hundred acres silently racing away from them. The sound on the other side though, he imagined to be unearthly. From his view it seemed a raging sea of smoke as if they were sailors at the gunnels of a ship watching a storm beat waves toward a beach they could not see. He looked at Kent.

"It's going away!" Kent said with a gasp.

"For now," Leonard replied. They both knew their homes were in the middle of what would not survive if it came the other way in this manner.

Before every hurricane, tornado, tsunami, or other natural disaster such as a wildfire or earthquake, there is always an underestimation of what could happen, or of what probably will happen. Conclusions about nature are generally haphazard or foolhardy, because we always gracelessly default to the status quo about everything. "It'll be alright," is the constant refrain. Generally, through after long spells of the status quo, something comes along that is *not* alright. Leonard's little family went to bed that night thinking it was all going to be OK.

That night he went to his basement and pulled out an old CB Base transceiver he'd found at a yard sale and got it going on the kitchen table, and began to listen to neighbors in the area. These were people he did not know. They were disconnected to adjacent road systems; in the rural landscape they might see each other at the store but would likely not have the adjacency of living that connected them. Over the short-wave radio, the fire had engendered lively conversation, where it had touched, who was burned out, and what was likely happening—and most importantly, one could deduce, when to run. The State Forestry had very little information by comparison. The federal managers were in charge and communicated among themselves, with a public information officer for the press. The next day, it was only the CB that gave Leonard the news from frantic conversations, that the fire that had burned down and northward from them had begun to back burn through the crowns of trees, south again and toward them. Leonard had learned from the CB chatter that the fire *had* back burned south up the Canyon in the early afternoon taking ten houses on Ramsey Road. The neighbors had thought they were safe as the fire had been going north from the small community the day before. Leonard knew when he heard that it was now burning east of Ramsey Road and through the powerline, that this fire would likely run up the westside of the powerline before it came over the ridge. Then the fire would begin to spill into the box canyon, which would kindle flames for a short while at the bottom and then begin to burn around, spreading and creeping up until there would be a point where, due to its ever reaching uphill for combustible fuel and convection, it would funnel the hot burning moving air into tinder dry grass, manzanita patches, with scrub oak and a few cedars all strewn over scabs of granite, and in a full on furnace-like fashion when it would likely explode. The explosion would engulf the canyon in its entirety to the other ridge that was behind their home, then it would come down on them. How it came on them from the ridge would be uncertain. It could be a slow creep, or a wind coming up on the side hill could whip it around and take the whole hillside at once.

The day of the blackcaps, three years after the fire, at the ridge top you could still see in the tops of pine snags, over a hundred feet in the air, black needles pointing the exact direction of Hell that came out of the box canyon like a hundred-acre flame thrower. The trees on the top of the ridge were charcoal black and glistening that morning when Leonard and Robinson had gone to the cliffs for a view of the valley and the Table Rocks and the box canyon that still had a visage of blackness, lifelessness save where the thick twelve foot high manzanita patches were making a comeback of green, but all were less than a foot high. Along the ridge to the cliffs, the still-evident heights of the flames in the top needles were frozen at one hundred feet above the ridge riding the still-standing trees, their clinging needles still melded to the direction of the flames the day of the fire, all slightly swaying like scarecrows. On their way back, he and Robinson had discovered the raspberries which were growing in profusion as they do after a large fire.

But midmorning on the second day of the fire, Leonard knew it would likely creep or burn fast toward the box canyon he'd been in the day before with Kent. The first day of the fire a state fire official came up and said they would stage a caterpillar, a pumper truck, and a hand crew up near his home and his neighbors' homes if the fire came toward them. The second day around noon the same man came to tell them to evacuate—they were not going to fight the fire there. Leonard began to get his wife and older son Charles to help him to load up the car, guns, papers, pictures, a computer, some canned goods, clothes, all piled into the trunk and the back seat of their Ford. His wife approached the emergency with a stoic manner not alarming the children in the least and made it seem they were not doing anything different than going to town for groceries.

Once loaded, they stopped at the home of their neighbor, an eccentric widow. Leonard told her there was not much time. She was trying to gather her cats. Leonard and Charles helped her catch one and placed it into a cat kennel with two others. The other, a fluffy white Persian, would not be found—and the widow was distraught bordering on hysterical. Leonard told the woman politely the cat would likely be alright. Leonard explained in a loud voice he was taking his family down the hill, she should do the same with her three kenneled cats and leave immediately; then he and his son got in their old Ford and left with little Robinson and Leonard's wife.

Abandoning one's home can only be a hollow feeling. In the car, Leonard was grateful for his wife's calm. By this time, as he got in the Ford, he could see flames at the ridge. They were running for their lives.

When they got to the bottom of the mountain Leonard saw a sea of fire fighters, trucks, pumpers, caterpillars on trailers, crews in yellow shirts all standing around. Leonard knew the drill. Anyone that was either a crew chief or a boss had a radio strapped to their chest in brassier type fashion. The army of fire fighters here seemed unaware of the fact their homes were about to be destroyed. Leonard went to the first man he saw with his attendant radio.

"There are twenty homes up that road," Leonard began pointing up the hill, "and if it were twenty homes that were worth four hundred thousand dollars apiece, you'd all be up there fighting it wouldn't you?" Leonard didn't wait for an answer and added, "If there was a Cat up there, we could get a line around all those homes!" The first man he talked to said nothing. Leonard walked to the next man he saw with a radio and repeated himself. Getting the same response, he found yet another radio-strapped fire fighter and repeated himself angrily. By this time most everyone had heard him. Then he turned his back on the gathered throng of men and women and stared up the hill at the columns of smoke.

"Well what do you think about this?" he heard a voice over his shoulder say.

"I'm damned mad," Leonard said, without looking around.

"Turn the camera on," the voice said.

Leonard repeated himself in the middle of the firefighters, as adamantly as he could, the newsman and the cameraman capturing every word, as Leonard explained the plight of the low-income community in the woods above the road about to be destroyed. Other neighbors were there and within five minutes one of the crew bosses came to tell him that he would get him a Cat to go up the hill. Leonard's neighbor Pablo had been standing there and heard the pronouncement and was smiling. Leonard talked to Pablo briefly and then went to his wife and had her take the Ford with their two boys to watch their mountain burn by the swimming pool of friends'—fearful, but safe, three miles away.

Leonard got in Pablo's pickup with him and went back up the mountain just ahead of the Caterpillar. He was going back for the same reason Pablo wanted to go back: They wanted to save their homes—their homes were all they had. Leonard's family was safe, and there was a chance.

He got back to tend the fire line, Leonard Moore and his neighbor arriving as the fire did. Leonard could see that the fire pretty much had crept slowly downhill and stopped at the fire line he and his son had built. The exception was on the south side of his house where it had spilled over and was about five feet away from a stack of boards that was next to his home. Leonard took a shovel and put the advancing potential tendril of house-burning fire out in short order with a little help from Pablo.

The D-4 Cat had followed them back up the hill and immediately, with deep throating throttles, began to cut an eight-foot line with its blade from his house to the north edge of the community to stop the fire from taking twenty homes. He wished Pablo good luck, as the man left with the Cat to see his own home protected.

Taking comfort in the fire line holding, Leonard Moore then began to keep it that way with a shovel. The line now holding proceeded to build a thirty-foot-or-more wall of flame as the trees and brush and duff began to burn hotter and hotter. Leonard was there and the line was holding but he had doubts—it was amazing that it was holding. His doubts about his decision to tend the line were pervasive but the fury of the fire and its roar overcame his doubts. He smoked Camel straight cigarettes and made his shovel ring off the rocks on the fire line. Leonard marveled that, had he not worked for the Forest Service three years before and gone to fire school for a week and fought some forest fires with fire crews, he and his son would not have constructed this fire line. More than half of his neighbors had, with good reason, just abandoned their homes. The roar of the fire and its pervasive wall around his home was fearful—yet it was magnificent. He had a small modicum of control in a force far greater than himself, but he had doubts. When he saw the wall of flames increase to almost fifty feet, he thought he probably should have left as well.

Then his friend Graham, whom he'd known from high school, had heard about his lone stand on the mountain and he took off in his pickup for Leonard's place. Graham evaded the National Guardsmen stationed at the bottom of the hill with firefighters and drove up the three miles of bad road into a forest fire to help him. When the six o'clock news aired, and the film of Leonard pointing up the hill and disparaging gentrification, he and Graham were clanking away improving their fire line that held through the night with their constant attention. A Mexican fire crew found them at two in the morning and relieved them. Leonard made the crew and his friend heavily sugared black coffee and brought a pot and cups to each man, he thanked them one by one and gave encouragement.

As the hand crew took over and tended the line, a burning tree fell on the house at five in the morning. The crew cut it away with Pulaskis, cussing in Spanish, in the smoking dawn.

Years later Leonard Moore remembered talking with their foreman, during a little break, about the Mexico beaches of Nayarit, the little towns of San Francisco, lo de Marco, and La Penita de Jaltembre that dotted the Pacific coast line when he'd been in Mexico fifteen years before the fire. The foreman allowed that he could buy small place in any of those little towns for about five thousand dollars. Leonard juxtaposed the burning wall of flames and his miles of uninhibited Mexico beaches in his mind that morning.

They saved the lower cabin, which was the modest Moore family home, that night but lost the upper cabin. This fire had turned a corner like an angry police car and burned back uphill consuming the red wood deck and when the structure went up in moments, the windows blew out on the side hill as fire and 5,000 acres of burning forest were so hot that the cast iron wood cookstove melted into a swaybacked hulk from a greater furnace than itself.

One of the fire bosses sought Leonard out as the fire came under control to tell him the reason for not sending help initially was that a hand crew had become entrapped and they backed off everything until the eight men and two women were safe. Leonard understood this.

The fire burned out of control for four days after it had started and took the life of a Cat operator he'd worked with the day after it took his upper cabin. The tragedy left the Cat driver's wife a widow and his two children fatherless. It had not been the Cat driver who saved the community, but another man. The fire had blown up two miles from Leonard's place in the late afternoon when the humidity had plummeted, and a slight wind came up. It raced a quarter mile in nine seconds, engulfing his machine and turning the young man into charcoal. Leonard had heard the incident as it had occurred when a firefighter had stopped in to check on him, and his radio became active—they listened as an adjacent crew witnessed what had happened. Later that day, Leonard wept for twenty minutes. He hadn't known the man, but his friendliness and smile were now gone.

For those two days Hell had come to visit him. Afterwards, his children and wife were fine, the house they lived in was fine. Even though the upper cabin was gone— a fifty percent loss was infinitely better than losing everything. Leonard had as well the realization that you can't be in two places at once. He had trouble sleeping for a couple months. He'd thought of the three days as miraculous. He should have lost everything. For months he thought of the fire every day.

Then his life blew up. Divorce had come out of nowhere just like the fire. One year after the fire through no decision of his own, Leonard Moore found himself in a psychic fire, as his wife took up with her boss—and for a time inside, Leonard Moore raged like a hundred-foot blaze from a different kind of hell. The vicious divorce had led him back to church, and he went every Sunday—having been absent for decades. Had he not been in church, Leonard acknowledged to himself he likely could have been in the State Penitentiary. His ability as a single father he counted only as divine intervention. He stayed in their small home, delivered children around as custody edicts required, had the youngest most of the time; the older lad Charles electing to move into town with his mother, but Charles came back to the cabin on the weekends. The black-cap raspberry day was one of a series of father and son episodes that let Robinson and Charles help fill up his life, the life he thought for a time was going to be as empty as the burned-out canyon over the ridge.

That next spring after the black-cap raspberries, a day came when there was the springtime flowery smell of wild lilac. Leonard took a walk in an adjacent one hundred acres of BLM land bordering the community that had not been ravaged by the Hull Mountain fire of 1994. There was wild turkey scratch in the duff of the forest floor. Around the corner, a roadbed showed a several hundred years of carpeted forest duff of pine needles laying over each other for centuries. An aerial view would show a checkerboard of logged private land in between the forested federal land.

A stand of Douglas fir shortly gave way to an eighty-acre stand of sugar pine. The jeep trail Leonard Moore was on was absent its usual dust with yesterday's rain and covered in pine needles from a uniform stand of these sugar pines, the largest species of the pines. The stand of sugar pine had the middle portion this mountain, and the jeep trail running through it was there for decades, winding through the heart of these pillars of pines, a cathedral that let blue sky into the forest. One hundred feet up they tossed out their wide-stretched arms making extravagant gestures like giant dancing women. At the tips of their limbs they were ready to drop their seeds from large two-foot-long cones, which looked like intricately carved wooden breast-like flowers, one hundred feet and more above the forest floor. Their cones could open at any time and release winged light brown seeds, all of them floating down like tiny helicopters in the air drifting with the wind, moving outside the stand to an adjacent clearcut, where the soil would begin this cycle again as the seeds sprout needing only water and time.

Like gothic church spires if you were to hover just above them, the sugar pines dominate this landscape. Three hundred or more years ago, another intense forest fire changed what was there, what looked like this stand Leonard had been walking through. The even age of the pine trees of the same size and approximate age gave away the ancient fire's story This was supported by an understory conclave of red and green vestures sprouting back at the base of the three-hundred-year-old large madrones that had burned completely down, old then, but sprouting as new growth three hundred years ago to become old again, these deciduous evergreen trees having lived for over a half millennium. Through endless cycles of the green bark turning red, peeling to reveal green again then turning solid red, the winding trunks and slick leaf twisting limbs resurrect power upward to half as tall as the towering sugar pines.

These components of the forest countering a seemingly static tale, if one would look and think, that the long ago is present and apparent and telling us to read this landscape like ancient scripture to see how it works. A liturgy concludes with the incense of flowing pitch welling up and down each sugar pine as it oozes out and wafts through the air. One ridge over and two years before this, a similar stand of sugar pine and Douglas fir are gone now from the fire Leonard fought, still blackened, and burned charcoal duff that took on a pall of death for a time. The fire that came on his home was no new event—rather, it was a renewal few understood.

He'd been coming to this stand of trees for years, for solitude: no hikers, no mountain bikers, no tourists; few knew of this place, yet it was less than a mile from his home. Leonard Moore went there often by himself.

He did not go there to understand forestry that day. Church, the day before this walk, was good. In the treetops, a wind began, and the pines began to move, much like raised hands did in the Church worshipping as he'd done the day before, but alone now, Leonard

Moore did something Leonard Moore hadn't done by himself, Leonard Moore began to sing out loud and alone, a hymn they had sung the day before.

"Hallelujah, Hallelujah, Halle…," Leonard Moore began to sing, and after a couple repetitions finally came into key and his voice lifted to the tops of the trees; then a heavenly wonderful Presence came over him, as out from his own abdomen, living water began to flow, a connection that surprised him at first. Then Leonard Moore was completely undone. Somehow he managed to keep walking through the stand of sugar pine, but slowly, step by step, and after a time, the swiftness of the living water seemed like a lifetime streaming invisibly out of him and into this forest in an otherworldly connection. A river of living water continued, and Leonard Moore was speechless.

He stopped walking after about a quarter mile on this flat bench of the mountain through and under these pines, to stand in front of a broken-topped mammoth sugar pine that dwarfed all the other large trees, lightening scars spiraling down its trunk. It was perhaps nearly five hundred years old or much older, but still with large cones in its top and a succession of them from years past fallen down open and dead around its base—and he found himself on his knees, not because of the remarkable tree, but because of the awesome Presence that was here and made this so, and showed him it was so; this Presence was all pervasive with the living water that was coming through his own being. For some time before this Leonard Moore had begun to see the matrix of the other sugar pines that had come from this large tree's seeds three hundred years before, now, all in a uniform age and size after the last big fire, that long-ago fire, bringing him to this particular day and an encounter and an opening of a matrix that he now knew he belonged to. It was ending on his knees and knowing what Leonard Moore did not know he could know—and then with all his being he knew. Leonard never had a doubt after that day. Sugar pine seeds fluttered out of the sky and down into a forest, growing renewal, as it had faithfully, over and over again.

Uriah's Song

IN THE SPRING, WHEN KINGS GO OUT TO BATTLE—then battle is all I know. I count myself dead beginning with each war—there is no other way, there is no wife. There is no life and I must end life that comes forward to me. War is not a backward motion. I never knew that I knew. But I knew perfectly when my company pulled away. No matter it was his will for my death, and not victory. I was always ready to die for this King. For I am one of his 40 mighty—I, a foreigner! a Hittite, as is my wife.

Our father's father settled in with these Hebrews who treated us well and many of us like myself and my wife became proselytes. Their faith now mine, and my faith is now mine own battle dress. Today is no different—except today I know. Just as these dogs before me will— I will die. But not before this one who charges out of the throng, and oh how I love spilling his blood, and cleaving half through his neck and chest—he never saw it. Now they see me ready again.

"Who is next of you—dogs? Who of your slime is next?"

He brought me out of battle! Battle! This was shame! To leave battle, I know of no other guilt I could be guilty of and not ask for forgiveness from this their mighty God. Because it is so vile and shameful! To leave battle. I, Uriah the Hittite shirked no battle, afraid of no foe. To leave battle? Sent from battle like some servile load bearer? Smelled fine food and his perfume in his palace? But not my brothers' sweat! What could be the reason?

This King is my life. When each war ends, but not until it ends. Until then my life is always Battle! War when it begins is a linear series of horrific acts. Each death an immoral, yet honorable action until war ends. This one is not over; we could lose, the battle King could lose, simply because he is not here!

That men would rally to his standard as the standard of the Almighty. My queen is death by my right and left hand both of which have the end purpose of my blood! I sacrifice a lamb for every man

I kill. Does this King not know this? He set me before table of feast and wine then bade me go to my wife? To my wife? When it is my oath to kill the dogs set before me? And there they remained and my brothers without me at their side? That is all I could fathom. I slept at his door and covered my head with my cloak and never saw my wife.

"Heh, you, you Ammonite scum, die as you run to me! I know your slime ridden brothers will soon bring your archers to bear. Until then, this is two of your hundreds that taunt, ha and now dead and the blood still spilling out of that one now! His tunic floating red now is a fashion statement."

"I want more of you, like a hungry man wants his dinner!" I am yelling at them, and three are running toward me now, one to the right, he will make a flanking move, the others come straight forward with lances.

"I will kill you all with these moves the Most High has given me!"

Their bodies shiver and make gurgling sounds. This is just a fact I report as if you were my Captain. We 40 men were schooled in the difference between killing and murder—I am a killer. It is so. Yet I have *never* murdered. But he the King? *Why does he murder me?*

I thought Joab could never do this, had it not been bidden by the King. I now imagine he carried the message that ordered this treachery—I saw it on Joab's face as if I'd read it myself. My brothers would never do this, Joab placed me with young men, first time in battle young men and when they withdrew. I saw them leave in tight formation, and lock-step unison it had to be on orders, as I led the charge and these dogs then quartered in and have now boxed me in, on this rocky field.

The King was angered when I refused to go to my wife. Perhaps he slept with my wife and brought me home to assuage this guilt? Yet, I cannot believe that. Did he not know that the most shame I could bear would be to leave battle? Fiends take my wife who bathed on the roof below the Kings' window. I joked about the

King seeing her private parts! Perhaps that was my sin, perhaps she will breed Hebrew Blood and connect to a lineage unknown to me. There is more than war, I know now that on this the day I die, I would want nothing but warriors for sons. Still, as I was leaving my brothers in arms for his table, I sensed something wrong then. A thing he thought I could bear. I can bear this betrayal better than that. Has he lost all valor and traded it for shame? Like so many things I must leave this up to the Almighty.

Ah, but those days he commanded us in the field! I would follow him anywhere and do his bidding. You see I could always see his anointing; the bright glow of his spirit was always visible to me. No matter the course, so I left battle hoping to be assigned a particularly dangerous duty.

"Oh! How, I love to side-step a shield and with a feinting move I kill this flanking bastard coming close—and he dies! While these two get to see me jump up so my sword can kill from the height of his shoulder, watch as I plunge it straight down with the quick stab which parallels down the neck passing through clavicle quickly and down, quickly down. Down into the vitals and as I come back to earth tipping, ha! the living falling corpse—it is back he falls. The air leaves him, and my sword is out and now, as he topples, I kill the other two! But the look on his face when I left the ground is still in my mind, as I now smell them all bleeding—and it is strange that now I wish the King was watching. "I, Uriah the Hittite, Servant of King David, and of his 40 mighty men I will go to my death with joy this day—as a warrior. I've never looked for rescue!"

My brothers backed off leaving me cut off, yet I cannot wail or keen as a woman. This like all others is battle!

I've known since I was dispatched from the King, some one thing was wrong, and if it be betrayal, so be it. That I've fought valiantly for this King no one will ever deny. This has been my immense joy when it was, I knew he voiced daily with Almighty, I'd seen him as a youth. When he'd put down that ungodly beast behemoth Goliath–stinking Philistine that he was—I admit it I could not fathom it. Yet I saw it with mine own eyes, I saw it at 19 and he was 15, and he killed the fucking giant with a stone from his sling! Killed him dead, in the dirt. I saw him take the giant's sword and cut off his head! The giant that smelled of excrement and ate raw pig's meat and entrails unclean and putrid and gargantuan as he was, he bloated in half a day after David cut off his head! Oh, how we rejoiced seeing the Philistine dogs run! When I heard later that the prophet had named David the anointed of the Almighty, before this mighty act of valor, I knew of no other thing I could do but to serve him—this David—and shortly swore my allegiance, to him and only him.

That it was his traitor son who infuriated me, was the only time I thought ill of him but only ill of wonder I could not understand. But when I saw Absalom dead my heart swelled with the joy. The justice of it, yet I saw my King weep and grieve. As if he'd lost an innocent infant child, I then thought him beyond human with tenderness that day. I, Uriah the fierce Hittite was moved by His loss and his ability to love.

"Now I see that they are sending five at me. Ha! I give it to these dogs they have not brought archers, nor javelins to bear! It seems they will try showing themselves men! Ha! I'll kill these five!"

I'm now leaking red blood. That was a little harder than I thought—my age? I'll have no gray hair after this day! Ha! This Day of my death, no old man tottering before a grave for me! I am a warrior and death has always been my mistress. That keeps me true to my wife! I've always been true but now there are other arms of Sheol reaching to receive me—I go there with honor! If there is resurrection as some of these Hebrews believe, I desire to march straight for it. But not before I taunt them more.

"Dogs! come let me spill some more of your entrails that I, Uriah, will make your whore mothers weep! Dogs that defy the Mighty One of Israel! Come die with me today so you will see Sheol and bark for even the darkest of mercies!"

These Hebrews taught me Job. So, *it is* He Who is Mighty— that tests men. Perhaps inadvertently but tests them, nonetheless. I am true to this test.

"Ha! now I see the archers being placed, and a phalanx of infantry with lances to take away my arrowed corpse. Ha! Today I die! The morning sky was red! Now a hot wind blows in my face. My doom is this day, but it will not steal my joy! My last battle—a wrong done against me, nevertheless. Through a cause of which I'll never know here. He has some reason not privy to me, and as so said Job "Even though He slay me, yet I will praise him."

Yet it is now so strange, I smell hyssop, I smell olive oil, I smell savory, and basil, and aloe. Their clang of armor sounds paltry, now I'm hearing distant cymbals, tambourines, and trumpets.

"Bah! I throw down my shield and pick up a lance! In thirty feet the archers will have to shoot to round their infantry! Now, I charge!"

Tree Planters and Loggers
Arm in Arm

LANDING IN A FAMILIAR BAR AFTER A LONG absence, and particularly a long absence after working your guts out for a two-month stint with no libidinal or libatious respite, is like a cool plunge into a pool on a hot day. It's winter however—deep, dark, January, wet and cold Pacific Northwest weather—and I've been tree planting for the past two months of the same wet wind blowing rain sideways day in and day out on the Oregon coast. I've lost fifteen pounds am in good shape and came into this place to connect with a friendly face or two. Hopefully, as well, a little female company, should luck have it that way. I have no notion of making new friends.

I have a full pitcher and a frosted glass of beer. It seems like a stake in something big, or at least possibilities as secure as a reasonably good poker hand.

He kind of came out of nowhere, appearing next to me on a bar stool with a lot of friendly banter, perhaps too-damn-friendly banter and one-line platitudes.

"I sure am happy-to-be-here," he says, and a minute later says it again.

"Sure, was a nice small town. Beats the hell out of Eastern Warshington," he says.

"Damn glad I don't work in the woods anymore," he says.

Then he started in on an ex-wife and how she was no damn good. I don't respond to any of this. I just sit there with my beer and freshly opened pack of Camel straights. I really don't want to hear any of it, but I'm initially not annoyed. There are familiar surroundings, I'm showered and shaved and not wet, or cold, and there are none of the same haggard over worked faces I've been looking at for the last sixty days. There's two women in the place I've not seen before; the juke box is playing something that feels good and I'm as close to feeling at home as I've been for a while.

He clearly wants to talk to me. Just me, and I've not made eye contact with him and have answered in only, "Yeahs" or "Hmm's," and stare off into the pepperoni's in the glass jar in front of the mirror of the ancient back bar with its wooden pillars that date to the 19th Century and a trip from the east coast around the Horn on a sailing schooner. He asks me what I do for a living.

"I'm a tree planter," I say, with more than a little pride, but still not looking at him.

I'm ready for somewhat of a smart-ass reply, as it is, I've correctly figured this guy for a logger and a bit of a redneck. Which is OK, I've been around loggers and rednecks all my life, and I set some chokers myself. But it is that I'm defensive. If there is harder work than planting trees on the Oregon Coast in the winter, nobody in their right mind would ever want any part of it. And it is true that there is this prejudice among most loggers for tree planters. It is an attitude that it is work that is beneath them, a lower form of work that has no appeal, and no class.

"That's Mexican work," I heard a particularly mean assed racist log truck driver call it one night. It however ends up a fact that rednecks or whoever, once they've had a day's taste of tree planting on the professional scale have nothing but respect for anyone who does it; and generally if they do it for a short stint, they'd never do it again, because it is too damn hard. I was doing it because there were no other jobs, other than beneath the oppressive wheels of the splinter factory of a plywood mill.

Rednecks are great, except any of them that turn overtly and ugly racist. Then they are not they are simply ugly and racist. I suppose my own fear is innate because I'm expecting this of him—and I should not. I'm still waiting for this smart ass reply to the fact that I'm a tree planter, but it isn't coming. Instead I get a run down on his last year as a timber faller and how he'd been in the big bucks, cutting Ponderosa Pine for one of the big mega-companies.

"Now that was a decent job," he said after chronicling a year's worth of dropping "P Pines" as he called ponderosa pines. He's looking at me most of the time when he speaks. I'm still staring into the jar of pepperoni and occasionally at the door, as it swings open for new arrivals. This is my bar, my home turf, and I've spent several months of paychecks in this place and I deserve, I figure, to be exactly who I am, no damn apologies whatsoever.

I don't know what possessed me to do it, perhaps because the same thing had been done to me, a couple of times by guys not unlike this fellow.

"I'll arm wrestle you for a pitcher of beer," I say, looking him in the eye for the first time.

"Well, ah, I, sure, suppose so," he says, seeming to wince a little and embarrassed. I figure this is fine and I'm on the high ground and whatever way this turns out, I'm ahead and will be able to end our conversation on any note and at any time which was my foremost purpose.

As I say it's January, everyone is wearing a coat and when I get up to remove mine, I see he's a little hesitant about this whole affair. He turns his back on me, as we move over to a table. I set down and position myself and as I do, he takes his coat off and sits down at the table and I see for the first time, that he has *no* right arm.

His left arm, however, sports a bicep the size of a large grapefruit and his gnarly hand is pretty much like a manhole cover compared to my own. I've got him on size and girth and shoulders, but I must assuredly now have no form of upper ground. I'm right-handed so this has to be a lefty match, which handicaps me out of the gate. When I look at his forearm I begin this contest with a suffusion of shame and look deep within myself to find hollowness and ungainly egoism as he wraps his fist around mine and as I do the same and start to strain against him, he pretty much slams my arm to the wooden table, and I was relieved as he was.

"You like dark beer?" I ask looking him in the eyes for the first time with kindness. After I heard the story of how he lost his arm in a logging accident, a pitiful tale of a log rolling over him and a stob severing the arm as it did. He said he'd got up and his severed arm was still in his shirt sleeve. I spent the rest of the evening with him swapping stories, neighborly fellowship, and buying beers one after the other.

Brueghel's Plowman Revisited

AFTERNOON ON THANKSGIVING AND CLAUDIA AND I WALKED up to the cliffs on Neil Rock. We had been living together for about six months 40 miles away, had the big meal at my friend Peter's and began our walk in the early afternoon. I had lived up there a year, two years previous, and this was about five years before I bought my cabin on that mountain.

I was in love with Claudia. We had met in a bar. She had sat down beside me, and we made pleasant conversation for about twenty minutes. I had known her in passing over the years, and she spent three weeks working in an office with me once. Some might think Claudia plain in a casual meeting, but she was a woman who could dress up, and, though not a goddess, she could compete with any woman because she had been endowed with a figure that was very complete. She finally cut to the chase in the middle of our small talk.

"You know, I have some really good bud back at my apartment," she said.

"That so?" I said.

"Would you like to try it?" she asked. This was the early '80s.

"Sure," I said.

"That ain't all I've got," she added. Claudia was dressed up.

The courtship was pretty much over that night. I went back to her apartment and lived with her for a good part of a year. It was pretty good too; we got along, and it put some stability in my itinerant style of life that was stabilized only by my presence in the bar. This of course was before I found out she was hooking for the cocaine she brought home twice a week. Our Thanksgiving walk was, well…it was before I acquired this information.

A pleasant chilly walk, the back way up through Phil's place and around the north side to the cliffs, that may have been some sort of vision-quest thin place when the Native Takelma Indians ruled the Rogue Valley before the California and Oregon miners organized a genocide between the two Table Rocks.

Once when I was up to the cliffs by myself, I found a smooth red-ochre stone the size of a quarter with a clean round hole drilled through—it had been hidden in a crevice perhaps over a century before. As I had walked up there, two neighbor children had been jumping on an outcropping of limestone and it had broken off. As I walked over the broken rocks, I found the little red stone. The limestone cave underneath the cliffs had a blackened ceiling of carbon an inch thick. There was a place for a fire and two other rooms in the cave. Someone hid the stone there likely before Euro-Americans came here.

This place, the cliffs, and the cave, are where the Takelma tribe of Southern Oregon came to worship in the presence of these two flat Table Rocks that are the geological icons in this valley. Perhaps they would be praying and giving thanks for a good salmon run, or many deer and elk, or babies who live past three. Here they made their red arrowheads in the lodges down below, or passed around pemmican, or smoked from a pipe while gambling for slaves, leeched tannin from gathered acorns and ground them into flour for bread. Neil Rock was likely the place for a shaman to take young men and fast them and feed them a potion and invite them to see. While they mapped with their hunger and the elder teller, all the places they would hunt and be able to talk among themselves and never be lost for very long because of the long looking above the sacred rocks and low mountains around Sam's Creek that are off in the distance. Back then, the limits of the Rogue Valley could be topped over the Cascades into the Klamath and off toward the beginning of the Great Basin in Eastern Oregon. However, here on these cliffs, that day this vastness was contained, and human parameters were apparent. Now, the hunting places and low mountains are all divided up into little ranches, orchards, small farms, and half-acre plots with mobile homes that divide up Sam's Valley. To the south of lower Table Rock is Medford, hazy and grey in appearance, with White City and Eagle Point off east and snow-topped Mt. McLoughlin defining the limits of the Rogue Valley.

We'd walked up to take this all in, while on Beagle Road directly east was the Sky Ranch where for a fee you could take a six-hour class and then parachute from an airplane down into this valley that we were taking in as a panorama.

As we were leaving the cliffs that day, a small plane began to circle over the valley perhaps a thousand feet over us, and two distant forms popped out. A bright red and white 'chute opened up, floating down slowly to the valley, and I had been used to seeing these parachutes drift down to the valley like soft floating seeds into the earth.

I pointed it out to Claudia, and as I did another form came out of the airplane with a white 'chute opened but in a strange manner, and descended straight down much faster, streaming and oblong like an arrow but still recognizably a parachute. Later, we heard the siren of an ambulance from three miles away and I wondered if the two events were connected.

We continued our hike, with a tour of the caves, and the next day back in town, as I perused the morning paper with my coffee, I read of a parachutist killed in Sam's Valley when his 'chute failed to open correctly. Apparently, he had been the parachute packer for the Sky Ranch. A week or two later I talked to a neighbor on the mountain who knew someone down on Beagle Road where the skydivers landed, and he said the guy had come down ten yards from a couple putting a new composition-shingle-roof on their mobile home.

"PLEASE GOD! PLEASE GOD! PLEASE GOD!" they had heard him scream from the sky until there was the muffled thud.

I knew then I had been there like Brueghel's plowman not seeing the watery crash and often I have thought of it as a freeze frame after that. We walked off the cliffs that day. As the skydiver fell, he had no notion of shamans. No notion of voluptuous girlfriends, or history, or anthropology. No notion of how good the Thanksgiving dinner was, or jobs, or money, or a new car, or what he did last Thursday. No notion of Brueghel, or Icarus, or William Carlos Williams. No notion of a liberal education in an Ivy League University. He did not have a nanosecond of wonder about agnosticism versus atheism.

The fall was not 20,000 feet, but 1,800—no time for a tight poem or flash fiction either. The consequence of his sin was gravity; and by him, it was not well considered. He knew of no contingency that could have stopped this. Since on that day, he relied on the rote of muscle memory for his own self-worth. He, having paid more attention for others, faced the parachute-packing- table for the last time. He did not think through what he had done—and it could not be undone.

Had he no Daedalus to warn him of complacency? Pulling on the tangled cords and knowing out of self-assuredness, he had not packed a secondary 'chute. Perhaps before he got in the perfectly good flying machine he was as sure of himself as our mythological Icarus—but he then cried out to God all the way down.

Still Life of Elephant and Schizophrenic Woman

HOT LATE AUGUST, A MONDAY IN 1994, IN OREGON, and the newspapers said that on Sunday a Salem schizophrenic woman in a sack dress clutching a wailing Siamese cat and a butcher knife came into the supermarket complaining that she was thirsty, then entered the soft drink aisle, grabbed a can of Coca Cola, and popped the top on the "real thing", still clutching the moaning feline and the knife.

She put a Winston in her mouth, sat down on the floor, and while lighting up the cigarette crossed her legs.

"My grandmother is a Satan worshipper!" she announced in a loud voice, as the employees constructed a barricade around her at each end of the aisle with grocery carts.

Then she started yelling for the police, who did shortly arrive, all eight of them, to spray her with pepper spray. Then she, with the indelible strength of her mental disorder, defended herself, raising the knife overhead in a Hitchcock *Psycho* fashion; and then the cops—the frightened cops—shot her once in the neck and three times in the chest, in what was termed self-defense.

This was partly or wholly the fear and loathing in willful ignorance of the unknown or unfamiliar, and, yes, partly the long-awaited chance to use a handgun—strapped to their sides on a fellow human being. This fear, loathing and ignorance manifests as working evil, even though it seeks to combat evil. You read the news daily and it becomes obvious something is inherently wrong about general human perception.

Within hours of this Sunday event, in Honolulu, an elephant was spooked in the circus by a nineteen-year-old man, who foolishly came up behind and placed his hand on the leg of the twenty-one-year-old pachyderm. The African beast (which was a circus anomaly, as most are Asian elephants), either startled or remembering an old injustice, tried to kill the boy. The beast's new trainer tried to intervene and then the huge animal turned on the circus man and killed him instead.

In India, a new mahout is considered expendable in these circumstances. This, however, was Hawaii, where no African elephant could ever be imagined as present in a natural state. It turned out that the circus man and owner was not the elephant's regular handler. The new man had a history of abusing the great beasts that had come into his charge.

The elephant, whose name was "Tyke," broke free in the struggle, sending circus patrons screaming for the aisles and in the ensuing rampage of the rogue elephant, cops were dispatched and took to the chase through downtown Honolulu where the lumbering legs began a pitiful escape attempt, wading through and dwarfing Toyotas in the street. Those Toyotas had been sent to this island by relatives of former bombardiers whose sights were now set only upon franchise and profit, and eventually the police took a high-powered rifle and fired seven times into the beast's neck to bring it to its knees. Animal Control attendants administered for an hour the final massive lethal injection as the animal screamed his elephant death-agony scream for all to hear.

The Clinton era gave us 100,000 new police on the street and a legal means to put more black men in jail and for longer sentences than white men because of the brand of cocaine being sold in the ghetto. In retrospect it was not much different than getting probation for smoking Winston filter cigarettes and getting five years for smoking Kool's. Meanwhile the cops—the frightened cops—with marching orders to arrest drug users at every possible turn, will ensure that generations will have fathers jailed and no progress for any social good will have taken place. In the hesitancy of fear, the cops will kill, mistaking adrenalin for the existential panic in a kill-or-be-killed scenario, and the unarmed and innocent will die. The author of incarceration of black men into jail for more lengthy sentences than white drug users will become the vice president of the first Black American President.

The elephant's eye comes to the forefront of the wire-service photo along with the quick action of the policemen who killed the woman with the cat, operating on protocol—as does profit on Wallstreet that can slam down death with the same effect—some of it immediate, some of it ameliorated over time. This lie, much older than the past two millennial shifts, disseminates itself again and again as both disguised order and undisguised disorder to fund a prison-industrial economy. Putting people in jail is lucrative for lawyers, prosecutors, judges, prison administrators, and communities that provide the service industry.

Seems you need on-call experienced psychiatrists and mahouts and the fifteen-dollar-an-hour job you can get (if you are lucky and sober), coupled with the $1,500.00 a month for the decent house for you and your children, and then add on the security deposit and the last month's rent. All this making it important to diminish any of the same rage of the elephant's eye and sanctify sanity in your own good right hand, knowing the blue juice of the lethal injection, or the police .45 is for you as well.

The conceit of scholastic determinism and 100,000 new police are waiting for systems theory to work out and looking for all who cross over the line—the white line, the picket line, or the thin red line that takes you to aisle number 4 for soft drinks. The weakest will be jailed. The strong will buy their way out—social Darwinism was alive in the 1990s and marching aboard a future rocket ship named ochlarchy rather than scientific social construct. Contention coupled upon contention rides in black and whites and in the afternoon. In America, magnum ordnance waits ready in the holster for the disordered cat-lover or the angry beast because of an unconsciousness of good as it really is, failing to couple good with evil as a pinwheel spinning in time, and because of division upon division of relative bureaucracies having paid only lip service to justice. Goodness, loving kindness, and beauty are ignored even though they may always herald the Kingdom of God. Whilst in the street, gangs of fatherless children arm themselves against an enemy they cannot identify, though it clearly exists, despite whence it came.

He found his first draft of this as a poem in a box on a yellow legal pad twenty years later, the last line had said: "My wife informs me after coming back from the store with ice cold drinks, that there is a forest fire about a mile from our home."

A Quiet Girl in a Gingham Dress

SHE WORE A GREEN AND WHITE GINGHAM MIDI DRESS that though skirted flowingly down past her knees, highlighted her figure by defining her waist and had a plunging v-neckline that bodied in on her breasts in way that let them ride braless in a rather spectacular manner. He thought her mostly quiet and demure as well as beautiful with her auburn hair, and she had flats that made her ankles and calves almost wanton in a mini-skirted era. He half-heartedly thought she was unreachable even though he knew he wanted her.

She'd always thought him good looking, if perhaps not athletic. He had a wry smile that would beam out under his mustache and shaggy medium-long hair. At least he didn't have a mullet, she had thought. And he always made her laugh. He'd usually stay reasonably sober until closing time. He had a lot to say, tipped reasonably and did not come on to her in an overt way. It was very subtle. After about a month he brought her a rose he'd picked in the park. She'd been dating a biker who, though not a complete loser, had a once-in-a-while bad habit of using heroin that always made her cringe. So when John Dalton asked her out to dinner, halfway through her evening shift knowing she had the next two days off, she smiled demurely and after pouring three customers their swill of beer, Mary Lynn came back by him and his bar stool and told him, "Why yes John, I'd love to go to dinner with you tomorrow night." He was surprised.

He took her to an expensive French Restaurant; they laughed and had a lot of drinks and she opened up and told him more than she thought she should have after thinking about it the next day. She told him about the second time she prostituted herself, but not the first.

She'd been in a remote gas station way after midnight in southeastern California on her way to L.A. and when she came back from the restroom after filling up, she found all the tires on her VW microbus flat. So, knowing the gas station attendant had slit her tires, she fucked him in her bus for a new set of radials. John had remarked that this was rape and not prostitution. She had remarked that, yes it was, but that despite her anger they were nice tires—and she needed new ones. He took it as if she was telling him about a fishing trip and that gave him a lot of points as well. She let him know that she was dating and planned to for a while, being 23 and not ready to settle down. But after the French Restaurant he made a joke about being still hungry and took her to a Chinese joint a block away for Mar Far Chicken and fried rice. Somehow this really endeared him to her. After the Chinese food they walked together in the park and they made out on a bench then he walked her to her VW bus. He asked about the next day and though she had plans, they agreed they'd have a date again soon.

The first time they made love, about a week later, was at his place. She drove the two of them there about an hour and a half after last call and he had stacked some chairs while she'd closed the bar. He lived down by the tracks on the north end of town. He rented a room in the second story of a turn-of-the-19th to 20th century house. His bedroom was facing the railroad tracks and let in nice morning light. It had been a day room for some reason 50 years before. The sinking foundation of the outer wall below had left a slight dip in the floor and it had a slant to it. He laughed that it made the beer cans roll into the corner. She liked all the windows and after a long kiss and embrace it was on. She had mentioned as they had got playfully naked that she did not give head. On that note he went down on her and made it obvious he liked to, as the 4 am train was under way out of the freight yard three blocks south of the house and as the whistle had blown and the rumbling got nearer and nearer she'd had an orgasm before the mechanical crossing bars had lowered while its bell began to ring on Oak Street, and two hundred tons of steel locomotive to the tracks became an impending presence and got louder and the house began to vibrate a little, and he entered her and they were thigh on thigh into each other, him on top and her legs spread wide and high, as the locomotive gaining speed passed the house, then the cars moving faster began a rhythmic clickity-clack, and they groaned and they made hot breath and both exclaimed Oh!, Oh!, and Oh!, over and over. It lasted until all the cars had passed the house and the train blew its whistle again just before the overpass of Highway 99 north of town. Afterward for a time—both of their lives were better.

Three Miles from Gold Hill

J ack Lapine's mobile home was on Highway 234 about three miles from Gold Hill, Oregon. Every evening Jack walked across to Sam's Creek Road, then about a half mile up the road, then back to check game trails and look for deer sign in the cool of the evening. It was 1987.

It began to be noticeable two years after Medco sold out to Amalgamated Sugar. Between I-5 and Highway 62 on Highway 234, where before the industrial clearcut on Medco land north and east Mt. McLoughlin, you usually couldn't catch a ride on a windshield if you were a hitchhiking bug. Now, fully loaded log trucks rumbled at top speed every two minutes from an ever-widening 250,000-acre moonscape-like clearcut being created near Butte Falls. This was probably less than half of the trucks streaming out of the clearcut effort; the rest were heading on down Highway 62 past Eagle Point and White City to the Medford Corporation's log pond, where logs were processed for the Medford mill that sat beside Highway 99 and encompassed a massive amount of south Medford, Oregon. The log pond had been feeding the mill for decades, starting out from a narrow-gauge railroad that snaked back up into the Butte Falls area from Medford. By this time the railroad was just a memory, but up through the 1960s, once a day the little train used to pull the harvested logs down the track and through Eagle Point to Medco's log pond.

Jack was about five feet from stepping on the other side of Highway 234 when a log truck rounding a corner and 200 feet away crossed the Sam's Creek Bridge doing at least 80, its driver blew the horn, applied the jake brake and made an easy and slight swerve to the right toward Jack. Whether this was intentional, or a slight lapse at the steering wheel by the driver, is unknown.

A walnut grove shared the five acres on the other side of Highway 234 from Jack's trailer with huge Queen Anne Cherry trees as tall as Tarzan's house, and Jack was not thinking of picking the ripe sweet morsels that would come on in three weeks like he had been before he saw the log truck seemingly trying to kill him. Jack dove for the weeds lining the ditch. He got up to see the truck as it started to close on the right turn just before the BLM park below the falls, and Jack was damn mad.

Medco had been the Timber King of Jackson County for 40 years. Eventually the entire railroad gave way to log trucks with cheap diesel and better highways, and the Medford Corporation, a public corporation that was mostly locally owned and unionized, provided family wage jobs for numerous families in Southern Oregon. If you worked for Medco, you had a job for life unless you screwed up.

Jack pulled himself out of the ditch, as dust from the tires of the log truck that had swerved over the shoulder was still pluming up in the air; he'd already started back across the road to his Datsun pickup, a beat-up monkey-shit brown 1968 job that sat in front of Jack's mobile home twenty yards from the Rogue River. The Datsun started on first crank after Jack had thrown a baseball bat in the old rice grinder's bed, and only one car came down 234 behind the log truck before the Datsun raised its own dust cloud as its tires screeched out onto Highway 234.

In the middle 1980s along with Disco, Amalgamated Sugar had, like robber barons from a Japanese Samurai movie, come into the Rogue Valley counting assets. Medco's shares were at $28 per share and the Texas firm lined up a loan from East Coast banks and offered the moms and pops in sleepy Southern Oregon $45 per share, and everyone sold out with assets really worth many times the selling price. All the large trees were now leveraged to the banks, so it was no surprise to anyone who knew what was going on that the trees began to fall.

Medco didn't do clearcuts prior to the takeover, but rather employed a system of roads, and many of the roads, which were onetime railroad beds, snaked through their privately-owned forest where great stands of Douglas fir, white fir, ponderosa pine and sugar pine caught the prodigious winter rains just east of the Rogue-

Umpqua divide with good volcanic soil from the Cascades. Enormous trees grew here, some of them taking the whole bed of a log truck and, while not quite redwood size, they were in the same ballpark. When you came up on one of the massive conifers in the forest it was an encounter with nature that made anyone, timber beast and environmentalist alike, approach this presence with awe. All the scientific definitions of old growth were met on the vast majority of Medco land, while in the rest of the Pacific Northwest, forests were being mowed down by the clearcut paradigm of logging that had been adopted by the notion of Silviculture, or tree science that operated very much like cabbage farming.

Very much unlike cabbage farmers, Medco's general forest practice was to base their logging operations off the little roads, entering into a harvest area by a road to take a red-topped fir here that had some form of disease in it, a butt-swelled one over there that certainly had a fungus eating up the first log, a half-dozen leaners on the other side of the road, and maybe thin out a clump or two of fir at the edge of a sugar pine stand that had candidates when the price of sugar pine might rise, so they'd stay. Three to five to ten years on, the foresters would be back sizing it all up, to do this all again. You could log a forest that way—well, you could log a forest that way forever. So, Medco's timber plan in the middle '80s went out to 2020, and that was not the end of their harvest—it was just as far as Medco wanted to plan.

Jack's Datsun had picked up speed and wound down Highway 234 that hugged all the bends in the river. Towards Gold Hill, past Lyman's Riffle, past Gold Nugget Park, past Ray Ridge's garage, downriver it hurtled like an imaginary little Sherman battle tank, Jack gritting his teeth and gripping the steering wheel as the little tires squalled on every turn he made, and from the rear of the little truck it looked like the Datsun was going to tip over and roll. Then on past the water treatment plant, past the softball fields, past Power House Falls, then a right turn into Gold Hill and at the Gold Hill Hotel Jack could see the log truck, a red Kenworth, making it through the town. Just as he rattled across Southern Pacific's track, he saw the full load of logs going north on Highway 99 out of town to Medco's Rogue River sawmill.

Medco owned three sawmills and its corporation had everyone working well into the next century with little change, as has been said already. It was hard to get a job with Medco: nobody gave up their jobs as Medco paid the highest wages in the valley and the loggers, millworkers and foresters had a well-oiled machine that was working toward four generations of legacy. They could continue to log this way—well, always, or dang near, with a little supplemental timber from federal bids, market ups and downs. There were rarely any lay-offs, and everybody always came back when there was one. When the takeover happened, abandoning this timber plan, meant a calculated end to all of it—Amalgamated Sugar made that happen in about five years.

Now Jack was hardly a Sierra Club member, and he fell timber for a living for about 15 years until a deck of logs rolled on him as he was making his way to a landing with his saw, hard hat and faller's axe—he was pinned under a log for a long while and spent a long time in surgery, and now had Teflon tubes for arteries in his shoulders. While Jack had left the woods, several friends still worked for Medco, and he knew the whole story and he, like his friends, knew it was the end of an era. Jack, however, could still swing a bat.

The Rogue Valley kind of funnels in between some small mountains around Gold Hill where the Rogue River, I-5, Highway 99, and the Southern Pacific railroad run narrowly parallel all the way to Grants Pass. Highway 99 follows the river pretty close, winding a bit here and there, and passes St. Innocent's Russian Orthodox Church sporting a billboard-size picture of Jesus after the Orthodox fashion on the south end of the church, that at the time before they built the new church on the other side of Highway 99, could be seen from both I-5 and a drive-by closer view of the Christian Deity from 99—where northbound, Jesus appeared to the left of the road in 1987, as you rounded a corner.

Jack had caught up to the Kenworth just after Gold Hill and laid on the little truck's horn all the way to St. Innocent's as the Datsun pickup was tailgating the truck, and only stopped honking about a half mile from Medco's mill, located at the south end of the City of Rogue River.

The Kenworth had only four or five big old growth sticks on it to make a load; the truck took a left into the log yard and Jack passed it on the left as the log yard opened up wide so the truck driver could see him, and gunned the little brown pickup as it brodied to a stop fifty feet from the log truck's path. Jack jumped out of the Datsun and reached into the bed for the bat in an athletic motion; the truck driver stopped, and Jack started to yell. Workers from all over the yard ran into the mill as Jack yelled and beat the ground with his bat. What he said was not recorded of course, and as mad as he was, Jack could not remember exactly what he said; he of course invited the truck driver outside the truck for a beating, but his rage, at the red truck that almost killed him, only cost the truck company a headlight. Jack and everyone else in the valley who knew anything about it thought of the greed that was going to make a way of life end for a lot of folks was wrong and undeniably this was part of Jack's rage.

As Medco's timber holdings were turning into an almost 250,000-acre clearcut, life was continuing with a middle class dwindling and the service industry making available jobs for only half or less of the prevailing wage of the timber industry. Farms were sold, houses were sold, people moved on. The contiguous notion of community changed to something else a decade after the dust settled at the Rogue River mill that day.

The truck driver's action of locking himself in the Kenworth probably kept Jack out of the state pen. Perhaps the smiling bearded brothers from St. Innocent's had been praying for the mill workers with their three-hour stand-up worship and liturgy that went all the way back to the Apostles themselves, or perhaps they'd been praying for Jack, but after his rage was spent in the sort yard of the mill, Jack got in his Datsun and drove home.

The corporate office that had its presence in the city of its own name closed after a good part of the twentieth century was winding down. The bankers on the East Coast who had loaned Amalgamated Sugar the money to create this large clearcut, had all their money back with interest. Amalgamated Sugar had a windfall of profit avalanche into its coffers because the assets of standing timber logged and sold were many times the $45 a share they'd paid. The Rogue River mill stayed open, buying logs from all over with its location right off of Interstate 5. A journalist covering this for a small magazine at the time, kept asking corporate men question after question, and at some juncture each of them would become unnerved at the challenge of the magnitude of change and at the obvious hardship that was going to be visited on those folks who would lose their jobs when the timber was all gone.

"Well, you know this is all legal!" they would say.

A small owl was the central character in a rage over timber. The Northern Spotted Owl would be happy in a pear orchard eating mice despite its natural habitat of old-growth forest; the friendly little bird had only two enemies there, the goshawk and an occasional barred owl. The advent of a checkerboard of West Coast clearcut forests, however, brought the owls' evening mouse hunting near created edges, where not only barred owls, and goshawks could dine on the slow-flying bird, but also great horned owl, snowy owl, bald eagle, American kestrel, sharp-shinned hawk, northern goshawk, red-tailed hawk, Cooper's hawk, feral house cats and others who had opportunistically spent 40 years of West Coast clearcut forestry adding the old-growth denizen, the northern spotted owl, to their dinner menu, and the small bird's population catastrophically plummeted.

The scientific committee that under court order examined the bird's plight likened it to the canary in the coal mine and warned that the Federal Government would have to choose between tree plantations and forests. Medco had done this for generations.

A plane ride from Seattle to San Francisco on a sunny day every winter with the snow showed the checkerboard square of clearcuts down the whole range of the West Coast. So, that was the real truth: the federal managers of both the Forest Service and the BLM stopped listening to what the common sense of the relatively small private company had known—to keep logging as a viable industry, which was the Medco plan, of a regular sustained yield of timber, that never cut more timber than was growing back. Log it that way and it could have gone on forever.

When the spotted owl became a threatened species, logging on the West Coast slowed to a standstill on federal lands. Private timber that was being meted out on the West Coast was cut for the market demand because of the gap the reduced federal cut created and our little owl went further in the hole as private timberland began to disappear at a heightened level. The creature's best hope may now be interbreeding with the barred owl.

The Medco Timber plan that went to 2020 had all its timber holdings in old-growth status. The locally owned corporation had mill workers, loggers, and foresters working and no clearcuts and plenty of habitat for all creatures.

This was an answer and was in perfect keeping with Adam Smith; Amalgamated Sugar, despite Adam Smith and the tragedy of the commons, was in keeping with Genghis Khan. The productive timber base of Medco, now gone, was irretrievable; of course, it would grow back but never as the base it once was that provided all the elements of a forest. The next owners would plan harvests from 40 to 80 to 100 years out. The characteristics of the old-growth forest would not return for 150 to 500 years depending on climate—if it were left alone.

The truck driver had wisely locked himself in the big red Kenworth. One hour after he got home, Jack called the owner of the trucking company, told him what he had done and why. He promised him the next truck driving 80 miles an hour that came by his rural mobile home was going to have a pre-deer-season surprise from his .300 Winchester Magnum. All the trucks slowed to the speed limit well before Sam's Creek and Jack's mobile home after that.

The Medford newspaper, owned by the *Wall Street Journal*, covered Medco's closing announcement, and having underreported what had really been happening in the community for the previous seven years, they prominently quoted the corporate raider's spokesman, as he blamed the firm's and the industry's demise on the federal listing of the northern spotted owl.

In Southern Oregon where most of the jobs at Medco were career family wage jobs, the logging jobs in the woods were gone, most of the jobs in the mill were gone, the forestry jobs were gone, and the jobs in the office were gone, and then the labor union closed.

Jack went on that same walk every night up Sam's Creek then back and often down to the Rogue River just before dusk where great blue herons that he called "long-legged guitar pickers" floated by on pterodactyl-like wings, and the steelhead would rise above Lyman's Riffle in the late summer evenings as the deer would come down to the river's edge. All the families that Jack knew were making do; with the coming recession and half the mills shutting down, they would be helping each other, cutting wood in the winter, and sharing venison and fruit and the nuts from the walnut orchard. And some of them, lifelong valley residents, would move. Move to Alaska, move to Eastern Oregon and Washington State, where the jobs were. When the year 2020 came around that had been the end of the Medco planning cycle that would have had all its past old growth forest intact—there was hardly anyone around to remember this.

Jack's Cousin, Crime

JACK'S COUSIN, CRIME, GOT HIS NAME WHEN HE WAS TWENTY. He had graduated from boosting candy bars at the Table Rock Market as a lad during lunch hour in junior high, to stealing cars and stripping the motors in an overnight chop shop as after-school work. He dropped out of high school his junior year to start post non-graduate work in a counterfeit ring. He was caught passing bogus $20 bills five days after his eighteenth birthday and got five years in a federal pen. When he came out after two and half years of higher criminal learning he was nicknamed "Crime" by his mother. The name stuck. Crime accepted it.

Crime was doing his usual drinking of beer at the Satin Slipper, a country western whiskey bar with a restaurant that served steak and baked potatoes and hamburgers and ham, bacon, and egg breakfasts, and broasted deep-fried chicken that had an orthopedic look to it when it came to the table with deep-fried potatoes.

Many, including numerous faithful patrons called it the "Sit and Slap'er." Crime had never been faithful to anything.

The previous Sunday night, Crime had a one-night stand with Christy Long, the wife of Richard Long, when Christy was out on the town and got a nose full of crank. Regularly, when Christy was out on the town and got a nose full of crank, she slept with someone other than Richard. Crime fit into the scene pretty much like he always did because he had sold her the crank. After he made the sale, he and Christy made a night of it because Christy wanted some more crank for free. They foolishly left Christy's little Datsun parked in front of the one-bedroom single-wide trailer home Crime lived in with twenty cars in various states of disrepair parked all around it. Christy's Datsun had been out front parallel with Table Rock Road and the brown Japanese car stood out with a day glow ball on the antenna.

Unfortunately, for Crime, Richard Long's crummy-ride up to his logging job had to backtrack and make a quick trip into the tire store at Witham's 24-hour truck stop, and they went right by Crime's little tuna-can home at 4:30 am Monday, and Richard saw the Datsun there with its day glow ball lighting up in the headlights as the crummy drove by in the dark. And that had explained her absence from their bedroom, as the kids were at his mother's home in Shady Cove, where she could have walked had she drank there that night as she told Richard she was going to do.

Monday evening someone had told Crime that Richard knew, and Crime didn't really shrug it off, but he had more than one man's wife over the years and figured it would probably pass. He didn't hang where Richard ever did, but they'd known each other for years. Crime set chokers on a couple jobs where Richard fell timber. Crime had sold Richard a couple new chainsaws that were most likely stolen, and that had been a good deal for Richard, but they hadn't seen each other in three or four years. He sure didn't figure to see Richard at the Satan's Slipper as he was fond of alliterating the watering hole's name. Richard knew Crime was generally there and drove straight to the bar after work.

When Richard walked in under the big blue and red glowing neon sign of a woman's high heel shoe that adorned the rural whiskey bar and through the door, he saw Crime at the bar about halfway down just before the bar's corner, where the stools and the bar made an elbow turn to the right, this side of the tables and the stage. Here every weekend a country western band played at least two Merle Haggard songs and the swing dancing swept up the floor, and cowboy hats were bobbing, and the tables were full, and the liquor poured over the ice like tiny waterfalls.

Crime didn't see him. Richard thought of blindsiding him and then it would be over; he could feel his heart pumping blood through his arms. Instead he took the buck knife he always carried on his belt during hunting season out of the sheath and palmed the handle.

Somewhere in the valley, sermons were regularly preached about how insidious adultery was because it often included the added sins of lying, and sometimes murder in the process. Neither Crime, nor Richard Long heard these sermons, or any other sermons for that matter, since they were children.

Richard sat down right beside Crime and watched him turn his head toward him and then watched his face turn white as he momentarily closed his eyes in complete embarrassment then blinked them open to Richard's cold stare.

Richard then somehow remembered putting a sneak on a bull elk once that was upwind of him and Richard had run around a ridge, got in front of the large animal, and waited behind a huge Douglas fir. The bull cautiously walked up hill but rounding a corner just as he saw Richard only half concealed behind the large tree with his .300 Winchester Magnum, the Bull had the exact expression on his long ungulate face as Crime had. It was embarrassment and his eyes had half closed and his head nodded, with an expression of, "Oh no!" but before he could turn his antlered head downhill for an escape, Richard killed him. Then Richard banged the knife down on the bar four inches from Crime's hand and then took his own hand away.

"You're going to need this," Richard said. The calmness with which the big man spoke was terrifying to Crime.

"Oh Richard, let me explain," Crime said, lowering his head again and shaking it back and forth slowly and rubbing his thinning hair.

"This had better be good," Richard said.

She Owned a Restaurant Up in Bend

"EVER SEE A HANGING, ERNIE?" Jack asked.

"Yep, my folks took me to one in Jacksonville," Ernie said.

"I was about nine or ten. Spent the night, had a picnic. 'I expect this will teach me a valuable lesson,' was the feller's last words," Ernie said.

"I don't remember what he did," Ernie said.

"Ernie, did you ever see a Grizzly bear?" Jack asked.

"Nope, they was all kilt out by my time," Ernie said, "Knew an old-timer from Jacksonville that had been mauled by a grizzly bear, he said he was out with three fellers and he got attacked. The bear bit on him, and bit on him, and bit on him, then he played dead and the bear went away. He said the other fellers found him and started haulin' him back to town through the brush, but he just hurt too bad. 'Fellers,' he said, 'jest lay me on top that there gray brush and leave me be—I'm a goner.'

"So, "Ernie said, "they left him there for dead. He said he stayed there on top of the gray brush for a long time, then got to feelin' better and walked back to town."

"How many whore houses were in Medford Ernie?" Jack asked.

"Six! There were six whorehouses in Medford." Ernie said.

"Molly's was my favorite." Ernie said.

"Molly's was right above the Hubbard Brothers Hardware store. I saw Molly about twenty-five years ago. She owned a restaurant up in Bend, still serving the public." Ernie said.

"Were you born in this house Ernie?" Jack asked.

"Nope, across the Highway next to the road that goes up the hill to the mine. We had a two-room house there. The mine started to pay, and my parents built this house closer to the barn and the river. This here house was built in 1900. I barely remember the other place. This is mostly where I've lived except for the War. Lonely since my wife died, had to stop driving last year. Missus Lapine gets me anywhere I need to go. My daughter comes down once a year from Salem."

"What? Oh, yeah, I fished a lot in the summertime. Limit on trout? Oh, it was a hundred back then. Lots of times I caught 125!"

"What did you do in the Great War Ernie?" Jack asked.

"Machine gunner," Ernie said.

"Mowed 'em down 'til they stopped comin," Ernie said.

"Ever climb Mt. Thielsen Ernie?" Jack asked.

"Six times," Ernie wheezed, from an abrupt old-man kind of certainty, and then he held up one hand with fingers extended and an upward thumb from the other hand to only waist height, and then let them down in an exhaustion of age.

"Last time was 1975," Ernie wheezed, looking off the precipice of his front porch, "I was 79."

The Other Night at the Log Cabin

HERE'S THIS BIG GUY, BLOND BUSHY HAIR, DRUNK, getting drunker; we're all sitting there drunk getting drunker, but he's pissed, apparently at his woman, waving his arms—she's turning her head and, that quiet coquettish smile that a woman can affect, she's been turning it on at every man who walks by. So, he's drunk and oblivious to it, or if he's not, maybe that's what he's pissed about. It's another one of those nights, small times and consolations, mostly just cheap beer.

That this incident happened in a Northwest bar at the end of one unpopular war as opposed to another is not so important, because the same things happen everywhere. The cost of dominion on this planet has generally been violence.

As I walk to the front of the bar it goes on and on. Bars with front windows are incredibly secure, there you are with your beer and through the window the world is far away and yet very close. You are kind of a goldfish looking out of a bowl with a front and no back.

So, the big guy goes on and on for a time and there's this small fellow next to him on his right. Neither is acquainted and as to exactly how it got started, I'm not sure. But the little guy very apparently got in the way. Maybe smiled back at the woman with the blond cat, who is, like I say, six four at least and lean. But he's smaller than that because he's drunk, we're all drunk, but he's slid over that fine line where words begin to slur, and motions and emotions often miss their mark.

It doesn't last very long, the big guy gets one to the body that lifts the small fellow up and off his stool, but he comes down out of the air swinging and lands a few before the big guy clubs him down with wild but powerful thumping drunk punches—he is a heavyweight—and the slowest heavyweights can do this sort of thing to the most adept lightweight. The time now arrives for citizens to come out of their beer and restore order.

Enter now another character into the scene, perhaps with a less-than-definitive role. It's not surprising how breaking up a small-time fight could cause more violence than was there to begin with, because violence hangs pretty heavy in the air most of the time, with everyone participating whether they admit it or not—the fight was really over when the intervention began.

So up he comes and out of his chair, not realizing that many heroes mostly are not really heroes until after they're dead. Those who strive for the status, and accidentally kill someone in the process are a statistic that is never recorded. Our new friend midway out of his chair is in full logger regalia, stocking cap, suspenders over long johns and complete with faller's pad over shoulder. Now every area is laden with whatever makes the economy churn the butter, but a working class that has to identify with what they do for a living is stuck with various images of itself that are pretty much taken for granted. You grow up around loggers, mill workers, truck drivers, and you learn respect for what a man does; you do a little of it yourself and that respect doubles. Forgetting it can get you killed as well. The fact that this guy was really clean, kind of gave him away to anyone who spent even a small amount of time on a log landing seeing the whip and pop of biting steel, high-revved chain saws, loud diesel motors and the scream of cables and pulleys dragging logs uphill.

So out he comes, every bit as big as our bushy-haired drunk friend, grabs him in a conventional headlock, and pulls him across the floor and down under the pinball machines. The headlock begins to tighten around a bushy head and a face that is red and surprised turns to purple and makes a gurgling sound, accompanied by the flopping of a six-foot body on the floor and the swearing of the small guy who is trying to break away from the two guys who grabbed him.

The "logger" finally lets go of his headlock when the big guy's face turns another hue of purple. Then he jumps up, giving a yell and a karate stance over the still-choking body that's flailing on the floor.

Well, this pretty much blew his cover, along with the red suspenders which were just possibly too new: if he had been falling timber all day and come in for a few cool ones, the only sensible thing to do would be to hang onto his beer and watch two drunks duke it out. That wasn't really it either; it was the fact that this "logger" months before had been breezing around town in a turban and white robe, of some sect, that had been imported to the West Coast by an Indian guru who was much more interested in picking up young blondes in his Cadillac than he was in spreading spiritual enlightenment with his lotus-licking benevolent smiles of supposed wisdom. So, our "woodsman," friend sported a karate outfit for a time and a turban.

It's amazing that all of that still works costume, an old device meant for carnival, has the effect of relieving boredom quite well. However, this was a bar in a college town and as working class as it appeared, it was not the Tolo Tavern out by the Table Rocks. So, the blond guy who still hasn't got his breath back and is flopping on the floor much like a just-gaffed salmon in a fishing boat, is still being menaced over by a bearded would-be Bruce Lee.

The little guy, who has gotten himself free and squeezed around to the back of the bar, which is the only clear and direct route, is making it to the door and probably wondering why he even bothered to get up that day. He gets to the end of the bar to hear the barmaid start yelling at him, something to the effect that he can't be back there and that he has to get out of the bar and not come back.

"I didn't start it, bitch!" he screams back as he reaches the door, then walks out, and starts to make it down the street.

This comment reaches the part-swami-part logger, who senses womanly honor at stake and comes out of his karate stance to fly out the door and catch up with the little guy who is now rubbing his head and stumbling by a health-food store, only to get blindsided from behind.

He goes down one more time, protecting his head with his hands, and receives a boot full force twice in the side. I'm still sitting in the window and all of the goldfish are nervous. We sit and sip our beer, the action having made it last a little longer, as Paul Bunyan walks back inside to make time with the lady behind the bar. A friend of mine who is not long back from setting chokers in the bite of the line on a real high-lead logging show over on the coast makes a comment on how dangerous it is to "think" you are a logger.

My friend could have snapped the swami like a lodge pole under a D-9, but the comment passes by the pretend Paul Bunyan and the bustle goes and on as if nothing had occurred, people steeping in their own inadequacies, intimidated by themselves, their nation and the paycheck. My friend looks up from his beer and out the window and then down again.

We both walk down to the pool table at the back of the bar as jazz is substituted for the country and western, despite the larger-than-life-size poster of Hank Williams on the wall, the smack of a rack of balls just breaking, clack and clank of the pinball machine, the drone of voices have resumed and also the clinking of glasses as cigarette smoke tries to rise to the speakers near the ceiling but somehow knowing its place here in a lower spiritual realm, only makes it to shoulder height. A piano riff begins, mostly men standing around, several women with ample cleavage to be seen. A blonde is playing pool with her hair falling down just above the tight denim that stretches across her peach shaped ass, the object of several male gazes from this side of the table as she bends over for a shot; the other side looks at the cleavage well-lit from the overhead light as she strokes the pool stick forward. A saxophone starts, stumbles, then makes noise turn into music, with trills, and wails then gets down with a piano; there's excitement over a big score at the pinball machine. My friend throws his head back, laughing a note of what could only be described as anguish.

"Ain't it too damn real!" he sighs.

We Were Criminals

MONROE'S GREAT UNCLE CARL HAD DIED the night before and that same night my own Aunt Pat who had raised me from nine years on, passed. Monroe's Great Uncle Carl had raised Monroe's Dad and his Uncle Buck after their father died.

Both men who had their Uncle Carl for a dad had dropped from a 1944 black night sky into Normandy as paratroopers, to liberate France. Thirteen days later my father drove a tank onto the Norman beach for the same purpose. They all made it back, after putting fear in the hearts of Hitler's supermen—Monroe senior to fall timber all his life, and Buck to run his cows every summer in the High Cascades, while my father drilled oil wells across the Midwest and Texas.

We'd somehow met up that night and each with the same kind of memories and grief in our hearts we drank beer with our pizza, at a new pizza parlor, that had been a pasture back in high school.

Cops came in later and thought our demeanor somehow unfit and being new and not knowing us as locals, they decided we were criminals. This decision struck both of us as remarkable. When the cops followed us into the restroom as we were departing, I had words with them—unkind words—and it left them bristling as we got into Monroe's old '59 Chevy with its sideways teardrop taillights.
"We've not seen the last of these pricks," I told Monroe.

We were '70s hippies then, and I hid our pot deep under the car seat when we left the parking lot. So, in this sense we were criminals, but we were part of a change that was happening, and we hated the changing of those we love, and we hated death, and we were too young to embrace it by any means other than defiance.

One mile out of town they pulled us over, spotlight on us and a bullhorn ordering us out of the car. I could hear the tremolo of a wavering voice behind the blinding light and over the baseness of the bull horn and over the roof of the car.

"They may want to kill us, don't make any sudden moves," I said to Monroe as we got out of the Chevrolet, knowing my thoughtless words may have started this, or at least seconded it. I knew they had guns on us—and they did, as we were very quickly being frisked.

Ten years later I'd been hunting ducks with Monroe's brother Dalton on Nygren's Reservoir, where we'd killed teal and mallards and afterwards, ducks in hand, we went to the old homestead, that his Uncle Carl had left only shortly before his death. The family farm had since sold to a large cattle company. They had not gotten around to razing the place, and no one had lived there since they took Carl to nurse him in his old age at Buck's place.

I entered the empty house solemnly with Dalton; we didn't speak the whole time we were there. Pots and pans still hung on a wall above the wood cook stove. The old man's long johns creased with twenty years of gravity hung in the bedroom from the hook in the wall. A dusky-footed wood rat had mounded a large four-foot-high stick nest that covered all of Dalton and Monroe's old Uncle Carl's bed.

Golden light diffused through the entirety of the old house that fall afternoon in the long empty bedroom, with a few pictures and a calendar on the wall from 1968, lit up from light though a windowpane, beside the old iron-framed bed.

There had been laughter and children and swimming and fishing in the pond. There had been family roundups, and Grange dances, and milk and butter business, and eggs sold to the neighbors. There had been courting from one farmer's son, to another farmer's daughter. There had been teams of draft horses with pet names. There had been a local grade school. There had been the long trip by bus to the high school in Eagle Point. There had been a buggy ride to church, that changed to car rides to church. There had been neighbors good, and those not so much. There had been each fall's hunt to larder up venison when the deer began to migrate out of the Seven Lakes Basin.

There had been a community of family farms. Most everyone sold off willingly to a cattle company owned by rich men, except Dalton and Monroe's Dad, and their Uncle Buck. The big ranch was sold successively over the years to other rich men, and women. The economy changed, and as children grew to adults, they moved on to live in town, to log in the heyday of the federal timber cut, and to work the mills, before that changed too. There had been three generations of this by 1977; and yes, even then Monroe and I knew all this—but the cops were afraid of us that night, thirty-seven years ago.

Both Men were Heavyweights

THE FIGHT WAS NOT ONE IN A RING, as a bar fight is not, as a fight in a ring. There were no rules or referees; motion and the narrowness of the bar and people in front of you obscured each punch. This was two timber fallers: suspenders, dirty hickory shirts, a faller's pad on the top of each suspendered shoulder.

Two logging crews just off work had been sitting there—choker setters, cat operators, rubber-tired skidder operators, the side rods, a rigging slinger—all drinking ice cold beer on a worked-almost-to-death sweltering day and now under a swamp cooler. It had started all at once.

"The talking part is over!" Richard said, and then he threw the first punch and it connected.

Away it went, arms flying and a few wild swings, a couple boxing stances, all ever so briefly, but mostly a toe-to-toe slug fest. Richard was landing regularly, his opponent was six-four, Richard was six-eight—both men were heavyweights. It began volley for volley, of big guns for arms, and bare-knuckled fists, and the Tiller Tavern was the arena. There had been no bellowing announcer to call attention to the dustup.

The Tiller Tavern was at the edge of the Rogue-Umpqua Divide due west of Crater Lake, Oregon, south of Roseburg, and North of Medford off the Tiller Trail Highway that made a half loop from the Rogue Valley near Trail, Oregon to Canyonville, on its way switching back slowly through the mountains running distantly parallel with Interstate 5 for a portion of the Divide. Lumber mills from Roseburg and Medford competed for a vast tract of timber in three National Forests. This large tract of forest trapped a sizable portion of the storms from the Pacific Ocean before they disappeared over the Cascades, dumping rain on volcanic soil to make large trees—very large trees, and generating biomass at a rate higher than the Amazon jungle.

Richard liked to fight. Sometimes after work he'd shower down, get dressed and go into town and wait in some bar for an asshole. The guy would say something, and Richard would say something else and the first smart ass thing the guy said afterwards, Richard would begin to kick his ass. He generally did this with a couple of drinking buddies. This afternoon was different. It was the crew. Squaring off now and trading punches and backing off a little was making both crews begin to scream. They were pushing each other a little and the adrenalin was pumped into an atmosphere that was building into a delirious crowd. Richard closed in on the man and received three rib-banging body blows before he stepped back and hammered the guy's ear hard enough to make it bleed. Then he backed off a little, feeling his rib cage sort of ring in a dull ache that was there but he was not aware of, as adrenalin was ruling his body.

Logging companies contracted to the lumber mills to cut timber from the forest. A simultaneous boom in housing in both Japan and the U.S. in the mid-seventies of the last century launched a domestic and export market that sustained the cutting of as much of the old growth forests as the federal government would let them— and it let them with sometimes merely a nod to federal law. The hue and cry over whether vast tracts of forest clearcut, being too much, or too little, right, or wrong took place far removed from each logging operation.

After a chain saw with a sharp chain and a bold man running it; the yarder was the indispensable tool for logging on steep ground. The yarder was essentially an industrial winch powered by a 400-horsepower diesel motor with two sets of spooled woven-wire steel cable. It was more often than not connected to a metal tower or spar that was 100 feet in height to allow the cables to span across an expanse of the just-felled stands of timber. The expanse of clearcut below the cable and carriage was an industrial pull of thousands of board feet of timber at a time. Natural-resource extraction is a violent act usually.

His rib cage still ringing from a cracked rib, Richard stepped in once more and gave the man at least two body shots of his own and then dodged an uppercut that, had it landed might have knocked Richard down, but as the other big man missed, Richard targeted his ear again and landed, rocking the man back and blood sprayed on to the wall.

The crew included a supervisor, or side rod (so called perhaps because they were generally logging the side of one mountain or another). The side rod sometimes was the yarder operator, who would run a crane-like machine often on tracks that could move to any position on a landing. The landing was a flat bulldozed portion of the mountain to store the logs and load them on trucks. The yarder could pick up logs sometimes from across two mountains and pull them to the landing with a rolling carriage on cables strung high above the downed logs, and the crew engineered them to the landing where idling diesel 18-wheel log trucks were waiting to race them to the mills.

The area below the landing and high lead rigging was sometimes called the "bite of the line" and working under it was highly dangerous, as ten thousand things could go wrong from failing equipment and lines to industrial brute force and ignorance. At any time of the workday the bite of the line, could kill you or send you to the hospital, if you were unlucky or slow. The cables sometimes broke and everyone ran or dove into the ground like infantrymen, from whiplashing steel and gravity-infused large rolling logs that would bounce end to end several times given the right mishap. Choker-setters were always in the bite of the line and if they were any good, they were always running. They were running uphill over logs, running down logs, creeping under precariously positioned logs to fasten a cable on a log that could roll any time. The choker setter in charge of all motion on the line was equipped with the radio and was called the whistle punk. The whistle punk would press a radio on his belt, and it would sound a horn on the yarder. Two toots would get the yarder operator to engage the giant machine and bring the giant timber up the hill with a spool of big cable winding and pulling at a steady rate like an enormous fishing reel; one toot would stop everything. The cables would slack, and a few moments would be given to make sure everything was going to roll to a dead stop to fix one hang up or another. The whistle punk had life and death in his hands if he made one mistake, like not seeing how all the logs going uphill had settled, and if he made a mistake, the life he ended could be his own. When the double toot went off, everyone was getting well out of the way. Caterpillar and skidder drivers could get killed many ways, like small timber cracking, and bucking back could send a spear the size of a car axle through the cage, impaling the driver in his seat. Loggers called that being "Jim-poled" and some were.

Douglas fir, a magnificent species of conifer, would range from four to six feet or sometimes eight to twelve feet across on the butt. However, they could reach fifteen or more feet across and were one hundred to three hundred feet tall. Cutting them down one after another with a high-powered chain saw to send a tree exactly where it was supposed to be was a calling for some.

Timber fallers every day had to face the exactitude of gravity with experience and intuition and sometimes a plumb bob to calculate where a tree should fall for three or four-hundred-year-old trees that sometimes could be over five hundred years old and pushing up to one thousand. The actual falling of the tree and bucking up the logs with a chainsaw afterwards contained the potential of a universe of mishaps. When you met a timber faller who had been doing it for twenty years, you met a man with a keen intelligence, witnessed by the truth he was still alive. Then again there was luck—sometimes it runs out.

The old timber fallers passed some unregistered test that probably matched the skill of great surgeons in dexterity, knowledge of craft, and the implementation of physics outside the abstract. A sizable number of them never got old. Ambulance and helicopter rides preceding funerals, or a life in a wheelchair, were common in every logging community.

You saw them down day after day, face cuts and back cut, down they go; you buck them up, then one day those true grains of wood fiber you've always counted on have gotten all mixed up—fifty to a hundred years ago they played a trick on you: one tree with five thousand board feet of timber, eight feet at the butt, goes down the hill. You're getting out of the way like you always do, to the safety of sideways and a little uphill where you're headed—getting ten feet away as the whole show goes creaking and predictably downhill. Yet fifty years ago, a little twist of fate had disease killing a tree next to the big tree you've just slain, and it was a pretty big one when it died. Your tree, going down, barely brushed the top of this snag as some extra weight had formed sixty feet up due to disease forming a conch on the back side that you could not see and has now made its fall shift just slightly from your calculation. The dead snag had been the condominium for woodpeckers for forty years. Now its top is falling in the opposite direction from your downhill-bound Douglas fir, and the snag's whole top is now spinning at a high rate of speed with a six-foot stob coming out from its side four times the thickness of a baseball bat. The top end of the snag comes out of the sky the same direction you are running and it spears into the ground in front of you, but whirling like a rapid snapping turnstile, the stob hammers you into a one hundred-and-fifty-year-old white fir and your liver explodes. They take you to the hospital, open you up and see this liver is less than Jell-O. Shaking their heads, the good doctors just sew you up and tell your wife that you have about four hours to live.

"Kill him Richard!" yelled the whistle punk from Richard's crew, as he bobbed and weaved a little as he watched the fight.

"Hit the mother fucker, Jim-pole the bastard!" yelled the skidder driver from the other crew. Twenty men entered a cacophony of their own expletives, laced with saliva and Copenhagen chewing tobacco and the small tavern shook a little.

The big man hit Richard hard. Hit him as hard as he'd ever been hit right on the jaw. As his head rocked back with the momentum of the blow, Richard's face turned into a wry smile. This was good, but he'd have to be careful—it was not a thought, Richard liked to fight, it was more like the heart of his being. Richard, since he was 17 was simply bigger than everyone else. The fact that this fight had lasted more than thirty seconds made Richard respect this man. The smile, however, was not friendly. Richard's adversary was seemingly facing the son of Gargantua in real terms; and even though he had the solace of underdog status from the beginning, the fact that Richard liked this did not help the man, who, though he had the capacity to knock Richard out, was faced with a six-foot-eight giant that was almost a head taller and had four inches of reach on him. Nevertheless, he was standing before Pantagruel and did not tremble. The light in Richard's eyes behind the smile, did not give the man confidence.

A timber faller had to be an expert at getting out of the way. He would generally work away from the yarder and crew and kept working the side of the mountain to keep a distance out of the way from the hauling of logs up the hill. Most all timber fallers started out setting chokers. If this were a feudal state, the fallers were probably the knights, and even though the log truck drivers thought of themselves as such, generally no one else on the crew ever thought of truck drivers that way. There were no truck drivers in the Tiller Tavern.

The logger crowd, though partisan in this fight, crew by crew, knew they were seeing the real thing. Richard's reputation had preceded him since high school, where he starred and was the big man in a state basketball tournament; though they did not win his senior year, that gave Richard a taste of glory and power. He could run, he could shoot, he could dunk, despite his size he was not clumsy, and he could shove people around. The fighting came kind of naturally. Since then, he'd been to Vietnam, where the tenuous notion of life began to walk around with him every day. He was grateful for every day. He'd gotten a finger shot off there in a fire fight and his first words were, "Thank God, it's not my whole hand!"

However, Richard was adamant about spending what he had won since then—and he wanted to beat this man down.

There are more deaths per hundred thousand workers in the logging industry than in the military—a statistic that has remained valid since the height of the Vietnam War. Fist fights broke tension. The two beer-drinking logging crews, one from Roseburg, and Richard's crew from Eagle Point, near Medford, were not having a Rotary meeting.

The workaday world of labor is unchronicled, in its angst, in its sometime heroes, and in its men of mythic proportions who never get their 15 minutes of fame. Richard began to bring roundhouse rights one after another at the man, sharply punctuated by vicious left jabs. All there was now for the smaller man was a defense of blocking blows and backing up as the torso of the giant moved forward swinging death at his side. This fight was a little like what death is like for both men for its last moments, swinging and hitting and missing and breathing hard and knowing pain from crushing blows as momentary pinpoints of light with an impending darkness unsaid and unknown that might not be darkness at all.

The crowd had really come alive. By the time the roar began, the entirety of loggers predictably picked sides. Richard's crew and the other crew began shoving each other a little, and there was tension that the whole place was about to erupt in fists, but the live action had gone down to one end of the bar, tipped over the cigarette machine, and was moving back to the other end. Everyone was making way. The owners never thought of calling the police. The police were all twenty miles away, anyway. Bodies and chairs and tables were being pushed and upended, and some glass began to crash—and two big men slugged it out, head and body punches thrown and answered and the shorter giant getting a couple good upper cuts but Richard landing more rib-crushing body blows, trying for the quivering liver shot that would paralyze a man to the floor when landed just right. Yet Richard's opponent was good enough to move and cover up and not let that happen; but blood had begun to flow from the faces of both men by the time they reached the other end of the bar and the thundering crush and bare-knuckle blows seemed to be wearing on Richard's rival. He began backing back up the bar toward the door but trying to counter punch from blocked blows. Then each attempt was answered with head and body shots, and then in succession a half-dozen clench-fisted blows from Richard's dinner-plate-size hands landed on his head and sent the other timber faller to the floor.

"Enough! Enough! You win, enough, stop!" he gasped, when he landed on the floor throwing a forearm in front of his face.

Richard backed off and let the man get up slowly, even though there were several shouts of "Kick him! Kick him!" when he was down, all let out in a delirium of momentary mob notion.

Shortly, though, wet bar towels for the bloody faces, were passed to both men by the tavern owner's wife. Beer was announced to be "on the house" for a little while, as insurance against further property damage, or any more fights breaking out, and everyone went back to cold beer before their long ride home.

The next day Richard had to work on a side of timber high in the Rogue-Umpqua Divide twenty-five miles up a long and winding logging road from the Tiller Tavern. He headed down into the hole below the log landing with all his gear in the near darkness of predawn. The balsam perfume of yesterday's clearcut of timber had exuded all night from trimmed boughs, downed logs and resin powering out of stumps as the earth's sweet blood; there was an unexplainable short-term exhilarating smell of the violence that had been done to the earth—it meant good money for everyone involved.

At the end of his day he would have a half mile steep climb straight up and out of his patch of fallen timber. He took each step down slowly, placing each foot exactly as he balanced all his gear in a manner so as not to topple ass-over-teakettle down the mountain. Each step was a wave of pain from yesterday.

The logging operation had slowed to five-and-a-half-hour days this late week in July when the humidity dropped to a low point where any spark from moving steel on rock could cause a forest fire. The Forest Service would shut the timber fallers down first in the early afternoon at one o'clock because their saws in the low humidity screaming through the volatile resin in the trees could start a fire; the shutdown of the rest of the crew followed an hour later at two o'clock.

However, before dawn broke over the clearcut you could hear the whine of steel cable, stretching, and screeching high lead lines and farther in the distance, the high keening of sharp chain saws and then the bang and crash of the first big tree of the morning going down to shake the earth as it hit, as the cut expanded over the side of the mountain. The cool morning air would change to 100 degrees or hotter just a little after twelve noon. Another day was going by and the big fight was yesterday's headline.

The constant loud throttling up and down of the yarder's diesel engine, the high-pitched horn on the yarder being set off by the whistle punk down in the hole with two other choker setters all interspersed with a clanking of the log loader on the landing to get logs on trucks that were waiting to be loaded. If the Forest Service showed up to fine them for loading after the 2 o'clock shut down, the side rod was instructed to start a shouting match and defiantly load the logs, and the owner would just pay the fine. The side-rod always put on a good show, often termed a "riggin' fit," and eventually the inspectors just let them load out all the waiting trucks. "Riggin' fits" were common for other reasons as well. Despite the high-power technology that had evolved from rail steam engines, and before that, horses, and oxen, logging often was done by brute force and ignorance. Things broke. Tempers were always generally short. Death and maiming happened regularly enough that it was common not to necessarily be happy in your work even though you might actually like it.

At one o'clock Richard Long dutifully ascended from the bottom of the side, his logs felled and bucked, with his sword-like chainsaw bar balanced on his shoulder. The wool felt of his faller's pad threaded through his red suspenders took the bite out of the metal in the big saw's weight on his shoulder bones. The high-powered engine of the German-made saw had been screaming through big timber all morning and was still hot enough to burn a man's hand, as it now hung over his shoulder. With his right hand in front on the tip of the bar, he controlled the machine's weight as a counterbalance to each step upward, each measured caulk boot step, up through brush and logging slash. He switched the saw from shoulder to shoulder several times during this ascent.

With the gravity of the climb and packing of his saw and gear, he felt most of yesterday's fight. Bruised ribs, (perhaps one or two were cracked) and aching arms, a shiner of a black eye and a cracked tooth—the extra pain against the ascent somehow felt good. Climbing, and using the gospel-sure-footedness of his caulk boots in each spiked step, up in elevation from eight hundred yards below and having to balance the saw and gear, he had to make his spine straight the whole way to balance the weight of the saw. Having to switch back and forth on the ascent a half mile down always meant a mile back up with sixty pounds of gear. Closer to the top became still more painful; the landing at the top beckoned as the sound of the yarder's engine and the disharmony of log loader and trucks all got louder. Sweat poured like rain down his face.

Although Richard didn't look behind him, Mt. Thielsen's craggy pointed top stuck out and pierced the scintillating blue air, and you could see part of Diamond Lake in the dark blue distance. The landing and reprieve were getting nearer. He was thirsty but would count it as imagination until he got to the landing. When his hard hat started to pop over the top of the landing's steep edge, and he got his chin just above the shot-rock surface, he saw a pickup twenty feet away.

His adversary from yesterday was waiting, cool and clean and grinning, having not gone to work that day, his arm out the window of the idling truck, and his own enormous black eye was swollen shut.

With his one eye the man in the pickup and Richard met eye to eye again—Richard was looking up at him now.

"Bet I could take you right now!" the Cyclops yelled from the running pickup, making his voice heard above the yarder's diesel noise as Richard's head and shoulders draped with all his gear now appeared, just above the shot-rock of the landing floor.

"You might be able to," Richard yelled back with a defiant note of exhaustion.

Still grinning, the man in the pickup waited, as Richard lifted his chain saw, gas, oil, faller's axe, and nose bag of other gear to the surface of the landing. Richard pulled himself up and over the edge. After all of Richard's six-foot-eight frame stood up completely straight, the pickup slowly backed up. Yesterday's contender drove off the landing in front of a high stack of logs, which had been a forest just a week before this afternoon.

Richard watched the pickup kick up dust as it pulled off the landing in front of the next log truck that was ready to head for a White City mill. With his aluminum hard hat tipped on the back of his head, in the burning heat, Richard took a long drink of water from his canteen.

Messenger

IN AN ALLEYWAY BAR WITH A FRONT WINDOW at eleven a.m., four days before Pentecost, Angel Adair had just finished his second pint. Angel sat in the otherwise empty bar with an elbow on the bar looking out the window. The bartender was thirty feet away, cleaning glasses. This bartender never talked to his customers. Angel had picked this bar for the silent service and early morning hours. He had met this man only once before. He would wait for Jimmy fifteen minutes more and perhaps one more pint. It didn't make much difference. Taking payoffs late, or early was just routine business. He'd never wait more than one hour—others in the union had to do something about the consequences, whether they paid, or didn't pay. However, the consequences of not paying were always more lucrative for Angel. Jimmy didn't really know that.

Angel's father had been murdered by company men during a strike in the late 'thirties. Angel was secure with tenure of loyalty beyond the politics that made many unions no better than the captains of industry they once fought against. He didn't care about any of that. Angel was not on a payroll that could be found anywhere— and not all of it was union work.

"Aey Dare, you mother-fucker!" Jimmy whispered while coming silently up behind the large man, having made it through the back door of the bar that entered a restaurant on the street.

"Now yer buying me a pint I know," he loudly jeered, motioning the bartender to bring him what Angel was having and laying an envelope on Angel Adair's lap with the other hand as the bartender turned away.

"You shouldn't surprise me," Angel said, deftly taking the envelope.

"Aey Dare, you'd never surprise me," Jimmy said, "Why ain't you at the beach this time of the year treating your wife to the lifestyle she's become accustomed to?"

"Because punks like you need to be watched, Jimmy... because of punks like you."

"Protection racket, union dues, or non-union undue, it keeps all of you from selling goldbrick jobs." Jimmy began after the bartender left his beer. "Unions are for people who don't want to work hard. Paying you to not run my own shop, is the only damn way I can stay in business. If I had to hire your goons, I'd never meet a contract, and I'd be back in Philly parking cars."

"Win some, lose some," grumbled Angel. "I pick up the money, or I don't. Somebody else likes it, or somebody else don't. You work, or you don't work," the big man continued, "or work and don't pay, and get whacked. Life should be simple. We drink beer. We all continue to live."

"I shouldn't complain," said Jimmy somewhat contritely.

"You should never complain," said Angel Adair.

As he moved the stool from under him and began to rise up, the long bar seemed a little shorter, and, bending over, he looked Jimmy in the eyes from six inches away while putting the envelope in the inside jacket pocket of his shiny sport coat.

"And if you ever call me by that lewd word again," Angel began whispering softly as he straightened up, "that word, which disparages both myself and the saint who was my-own-mother, I will stick an ice pick in your throat in a back alley some night, when-you-never-know-I'm-there ."

Angel, now standing and straight, lifted his right hand slowly up above Jimmy's shoulder, as if it were a benediction.

"This, I now know, you understand." He said pleasantly and loudly, and then he brought a hand the size of a dinner plate down and delicately flicked a piece of imaginary lint from Jimmy's shoulder. Angel left his newly poured untouched beer on the bar without paying for Jimmy's beer, which had just arrived. Then the big man walked out into the alleyway where traffic from the street, thirty feet from the door, made the same noise it had yesterday. Angel Adair had to stop and see Johnny Rose at his club three blocks away and he'd made a mental note to stop for a package of chops at Rossellini's meat market across the street.

He got in his Lincoln and started it up after a respite of settling into the leather seat. Wheeling onto Eighth Street then catching a green light at Lawrence Street, he glided the big black Continental into a right turn and onto Lawrence. The big motor whined down on the next block, and Angel braked and arrived in front of Johnny's Club.

The club was empty except for the bartender and Johnny who was sitting on the last stool of the U-shaped bar in a manner so he could see whoever came in.

"A whiskey for my friend," Johnny said to the bartender as Angel came around the bar.

"A beer back," said Angel, taking a seat next to Johnny. Angel slid the envelope out of his coat and onto the bar in front of Johnny, who moved it up and into the inside pocket of his tweed coat. They settled as the drinks arrived and could look into a mirror on the wall island that was the exact opposite on the other side with rows of liquor for three bartenders on busy nights.

"How's about a vacation for two weeks?" Johnny said, "then some house painting in July and August?" Johnny slipped another envelope back to Angel. "Here's ten G's for the vacation, we'll talk after the Fourth."

"You bet Johnny!" Angel said. He downed the whiskey, and then the beer in two swallows.

"Thanks, Johnny" Angel said, as he got up to leave. He knew the short conversation meant he'd have to kill someone after the Fourth of July, and he would give it no thought until the fifth. There were chops at Rossellini's.

Now I Know that I Did Not Know

AH, HE WAS ALWAYS LAUGHING, and it infuriated me. It seemed he didn't care about anything other than hunting and fishing and his damn goats. I could never get him to help with the wheat more than an hour. I hated the damn goats.

Oh, he'd take plenty when harvest came, and leave me some dried goat meat, or venison three months later—oh he'd always give something, but he wouldn't work much. Bragged about it too, said he'd figured it took him about seventeen hours a week of scuffing up his feet to get what they needed to eat, and sometimes that was just fishing!

I admit I took it easy in the winter, but if I didn't work ten to sixteen hours a day, we wouldn't eat every day of the year, and well, just look at what I'd done I'd built irrigation canals, a barn, our home, the wheat fields and the vineyards, and wells that made such a difference. I have slaves, my sons dress in cotton, and we employ people at looms for trading cloth for things we do not grow, and we have schedules, and we always know where the children are. And I made dams and diverted water from the streams to dry land and the crops that we grew! There seemed to be no end to how productive we could be!

Abel was never where he was supposed to be. Oh, you'd hear the bells on his goats, but you might not see him for three days after you first heard them. I'd hear from my friends that they'd talked to him long before he'd come see me, and once when I went to visit he'd told me where he'd be and when I got there, he'd left his goats in a valley and went off hunting for three days.

"You knew I'd come back," he said the next time I saw him and complained, "You could have stayed, and my wife would have fed you cheese and berry pies and you could have fished by the pool."

I was always frustrated with him, if not angry. When we were told by our Father to make offerings, I took what I'd made with my own two hands: sheaves of wheat, clay pots, vegetables from the garden, nuts, and fruits from the orchards.

Abel killed his three best kid goats. When the offering was over, he became a cloud of white and yellow light that day and had favor with Him. I had worked for twenty years to get wheat like that; the vegetables and fruit were from a garden and groves I tended for twenty-five years; the fruit and nuts had no more wild bitter taste but were sweet and good. I was empty and felt what I had done with arduous work to please Him was nothing in His eyes. Abel gave nothing he himself had made and always He was wild and fierce. Abel ran to that and what he has spawned is wild and fierce, and I somehow wanted to make war on that. Thinking order and homes and buildings and clean clothes more important than—well, I thought it more important than passionate love.

I was jealous, wrinkled-up jealous with envy I was, I admit it full well. You see I made lamps and could work with my hands and was with my wife when it was dark; and he made fires and holed up in smoky holes in the mountains and lived in skin tents on the plains. Yet, He loved him and showered him with blessings every day and the herds were plentiful, and he'd begun using his goats just for milk, because he hunted most every day but one, and he had honey and meat and the goats had mostly become his pets.

How many times did I see him in the forest when we were boys, when we were supposed to be gathering mushrooms, and instead he'd be looking up with his arms raised and worshipping?

Our Father had told me that was the source of his favor, nevertheless, after the offering I could not take it anymore really. I am sorry, I did not know. There was a reality that he perceived that was more real than what I knew, and though it's no excuse, that is why in the end I asked what I asked about my brother. Yes, it was an envious lie. My bitterness betrayed me.

Now I know that I did not know. He wanted only me, rather than the good things I might make, or do. I've lost everything, most of my family has died from plague—now my skin is white as sand and my sorrow never ceases. I must go northeast and build a city where there is no one.

I have begun to wander. He will see me again someday, and I hope that I can do what is right despite the never-ending memory that, when I saw my brother in the field next to the pool looking to heaven and laughing with joy—I crushed his skull with a rock.

Easter Sunday Afternoon

H E WAS STOOPED OVER AND ABOUT five-foot-five on a freeway entrance on I-5 northbound, with two good-sized paper grocery bags. Bundled up as he was, you could not discern by a scraggly grey-streaked beard; could have easily been fifty or older, but, stocking-capped, it was hard to tell.

"Oh thanks, oh thanks," He said.

"I need a seven-mile ride!" He said.

Clear blue sky met us both and the twenty-year-old Ford picked up to freeway speed, and he was settling in with his bags at his feet. There were four, quart bottles of Rainer Ale.

"Warming up eh?" He said.

"Well yes, and its Easter," I say, and I told him I'd just been to church, told him the Pastor preached the Road to Emmaus, and…

"Luke 24!" He said.

"They were walking with Jesus!" He said.

"Didn't know it was Him!" He said.

I thought of stumbling over some point this Pastor had made, then I stopped. He knew scripture; I listened.

"Didn't know, until they broke bread with him, Ha!" He said, slapping his knee.

"Got me a bridge up here I like!" He said, almost growling.

"Stays nice and dry, I can have a little fire, and nobody sees the smoke." He said.

"I stopped being able to live inside about fifteen years ago." He said.

"Don't know why, I can't live inside. I do pretty good. I worry in the winter that my feet will freeze." He said.

"I do pretty good though, see my way around, find places like this bridge." He said.

"Haven't been rolled in two years." He said.

"I can't live inside." He said.

"Wrap my feet with paper on winter nights." He said.

"I'm afraid in the winter my feet might freeze." He repeated.

"My feet froze seven years ago, lost one toe." He said.

"But it's getting warm now." He said.

"I do pretty good." He said.

When we arrived at his bridge, I got off onto the freeway shoulder with my Ford, and we talked for a while. My heart burned. I remembered I'd just bought a box of oranges. I got out and retrieved a dozen to a plastic bag from the trunk, I'd just done laundry and there were wool socks on top of the laundry basket, I put those in with the oranges and I found a twenty and gave him that too.

"He is risen!" I said.

"He is risen indeed!" He said, then vanished down under a roadbed bridge home.

Elmore

TOMMY CAMP WAS THE MANAGER OF THE ROCKING R and he wasn't a cowboy. He'd been in Real Estate for twenty years and when Elmore Stott, asked him to manage the ranch as a bean counter, after Elmore had bought up the last family farm he could get and consolidated 20,000 acres of irrigated farms, forest woodland and a loose road system that connected and salamandered around the South Fork, Tommy took the job and started wearing a cowboy hat and cowboy boots, and he started making the place earn money for Elmore with 2,000 head of Hereford cows and three ranch hands with families, all of whom were top cowboys—that simple business model was the start, and it began to grow.

Elmore came out every weekend and worked, drove a tractor, and helped manage land. He let Tommy do business, but he bought and sold cows, taking his cowboy's advice from time to time. Altogether he'd bought twenty family farms. Some of them still existed as a ranch house only and a barn as the children began to migrate off the land about the time the salmon runs played out. Elmore turned the Gerard's ranch house into his home and though it was pedestrian enough not to attract attention, the driveway got paved, the place landscaped nicely, and it became Elmore's. There were still four other big ranches, but the biggest wasn't half the size of the Rocking R and it was up the North Fork where they raised shorthorns. They'd gotten to the size they are as a corporation doing exactly what Elmore had done. But Elmore had a lot more money than their corporate board had. Most of them had never been within 300 miles of the place. Elmore lived there. Elmore also was aware that he had finished destroying a rural community that had been viable for almost 100 years. He didn't think twice about it though. He offered them a fair price and made deals so they could exit the property in a manner that allowed them to take care of all the business they needed to. He didn't raze any of the homes, but he let them run down on their own. Most all the children of the farmers who sold out had a lifelong bitterness about it, but they did not want to stay on the land. When the timber industry was vibrant—family wage jobs and a place in town close to the schools made sense. Some who wanted to stay, worked for Elmore for a time. Every time Elmore closed a deal on a family farm, he had a little regret. As the years wore on, he admitted to himself that the reason he pursued buying up the lion's share of the little valley and erasing a community was because, well it was because he was a little greedy.

Elmore was a kingmaker: he owned six newspapers and half the state's representatives, had visits from limousines bringing U.S. senators, and though the governor never came out there, when he became a senator he did. Elmore had made all his money when he was the head of the State Highway Commission had Tommy Camp's father buying property one year before the state built any highway, and he did that for thirty years. He'd been gone from the Highway Commission for almost twenty years by this time.

"Well now, why do you want to buy *The Quotidian*—really?" Elmore asked.

Wednesday morning, he was on the phone negotiating the sale of one of his newspapers.

"Mr. Stott," the inquiring voice began, "We see *The Quotidian* adding to our networks demographics at a key time and place and intend to ramp up circulation aggressively."

"Really, that so?" Elmore asked.

He let the East Coast lawyer go on talking and decided not to listen for a while. The truth was Elmore Stott, though he owned newspapers for political purposes himself, he owned newspapers mostly because he liked their smell and the sound the press made when it was rolling, and he liked pressmen running around playing the big machines like a piano, and he liked seeing the stacks of clean-smelling paper come out bundled and off to the delivery room. He didn't really care anymore what the paper printed because he knew it was all going to change. His first job that was not farm related, he'd grown up on a gentleman's farm, had been setting type from a California job case in his father's newspaper on the road to the Oregon coast. He seldom liked editors, and reporters were to him much like flies. Except for about three of whom he still played cards with on occasion and who knew never to write anything about him, or his business, or the politicians he owned unless he asked them to. They also knew he'd selectively throw them scoops from time to time, some in Elmore's interest, and often just because he knew what was going on. Elmore had been a full Colonel in World War II; he'd been behind the lines in logistics, sending trucks, sending tanks, moving supplies and on the radio reporting to the great generals of the Allied invasion every day and sometimes through the night. As the war drew on, he knew pretty much every battle and where things were and what was needed. He never fired a shot and though his unit for a time received some artillery fire from the Germans, he was never really in harm's way. He saw, however, the carnage—the American and British dead and wounded. He saw them come in every day.

A national news network was buying and consolidating a conservative spin on key elements of demography. Elmore had figured that out and though he was neither fish nor fowl about most of their politics, because as the kingmaker, he knew that newspaper was in a liberal enclave and despite any attempt at propaganda, that would not likely change. He knew they wanted it for that purpose— and he knew that purpose would likely fail. When the lawyer stopped talking and adamantly told him what a great deal this was, Elmore knew it was his turn to talk not by what he'd said, but by the tone of the man's voice.

"Well your offer may be wonderful to you," he sighed, "but if you really want to buy *The Quotidian* it will cost you exactly a million dollars more than what you've offered me. Thanks for your interest though." Then Elmore hung up on him.

Just before noon they called again and haggled a little and Elmore's price went up another $250,000, Elmore liked owning newspapers—this many small newspapers was a power base: they ran themselves and he influenced every election. He had lunch with his wife at the white table in the kitchen that looked down on the pastures and the creek, and then called about a bull sale that was happening down in Red Bluff, and spoke to Tommy on the phone. He took one call from the senator and then made the decision to go to Red Bluff next week and buy two bulls—one for himself and one for the senator.

Wednesday afternoon, about 5:30 in late May of 1974, after one beer at the Tavern, Elmore had gone to an ATM, 10 miles down the road and took out $800 in cash to buy a trailer. Early Thursday morning, he planned to use the new trailer to haul yew-wood posts he'd gotten for corner posts on the Ranch and was going to have two ranch hands move them the next day. As he left the ATM a man in a sweatshirt and a black stocking cap pulled a knife and demanded his money.

"You don't need to do this," Elmore said, and reached into his pants pocket with his left hand and pulled out a twenty and held the money out toward the young man. He slowly took the twenty then cut Elmore's hand and then raised back his head and laughed.

"Give me the rest, you old son-of-a-bitch!" the robber screamed.

Elmore had his right hand in his coat pocket and took his Ruger .22 revolver out of his coat pocket just as the man laughed, and shot him twice in the eye, as the last word dropped from his mouth.

Elmore then walked to a pay phone, dropped in a coin, and called 911. The man writhed on the ground for a little while, and then laid still about the time the dispatcher answered, with blood pooling on the asphalt around the body.

"What is your emergency?" the dispatcher asked.

"I was afraid for my life." Elmore said, before he told the dispatcher who he was and where he was.

"Please send an ambulance and please send it quickly," Elmore said. Then he hung up and wrapped his hand with his handkerchief.

When the police arrived with the ambulance, Elmore had his gun laid on the ground and told them he had nothing to say, and that he'd communicate only with his lawyer present—Elmore's second call had been to his lawyer who gave explicit instructions. The cops took his gun and put cuffs on him and took Elmore away. By the time they arrived at the station, his lawyer and the sheriff were already there.

The sheriff, had received a call from the lawyer, had left his wife mid-dinner ten miles away and was now admonishing his deputies to take the cuffs off.

"I'm terribly sorry about this, Mr. Stott!" came out of his mouth a half dozen times.

At about 7 p.m. on Friday, they released him to his lawyer who drove him home. When Elmore got home at 7:30 he threw up for about 10 minutes. There had been no more questions since Elmore had the last interview with the sheriff's department with his lawyer present on Thursday. They had brought his gun back on Friday afternoon. The lawyer told him there was likely to be a couple more interviews with the D.A.

On Saturday Elmore turned 75. There had been no mention of the shooting in any of the area's papers other than a brief description in the police log. Elmore, a split second before the man cut him, had decided to give him all the money, and a moment later it was over. Three weeks later his demands were met, and Elmore sold the newspaper and began to search for more farms to buy.

Now, Let-Me-Tell-You-This-Story...

I WAS IN PETER'S CABIN IN SOUTHERN OREGON, in the summer of 1981. Peter had finished at Crosier Seminary in 1965 and having done a stint as a chaplain in the Navy, or maybe it was the Army, he declined to be ordained, and went to work selling books for New Directions.

In 1967, he'd been chatting up bookstores for James Laughlin, and he stopped in San Francisco—took LSD, and tried briefly to become King of the Hippies. Soon realizing there were too many pretenders to the throne, he then retreated to Southern Oregon, where he bought a very small cabin in the woods and went on forays for *Amanita muscaria* mushrooms every fall and for *Amanita pantherinas* every spring on the Oregon coast or in the mountains. He'd dry hundreds of them and step into an altered reality most every day, then run ten miles so in his mid-forties he looked like an athlete in his twenties.

Peter had an estranged wife in Northern California and a young daughter and was dating a nurse from the psych ward in a Medford hospital. When I met him, I'd rented a small cabin about a half-mile from his. The first time I was in his cabin, on a round oak dining table was a copy of Wasson's, *Soma: Divine Mushroom of Immortality*, an ethno-mycological study—the cover a stark-white layout with two bright red *Amanita muscaria* mushrooms with white spots.

You will see this entheogenic mushroom in illustrations of Grimm's fairy tales and even Disney's Snow White. Wasson's contention is that this mushroom was the ancient Vedic intoxicant soma and as an entheogenic had been instrumental in prehistoric world religion, and that it is widely held now, as a naturalistic explanation of early religion.

The summer after college in 1973, I apartment-sat my English professor's small place in Cambridge, Massachusetts, where I read this book, and Peter, impressed that I knew anything about it, shortly over a few weeks proceeded to let me sample, his *Amanita pantherinas*, which were not red but the color of gold leaf when the light and forest moisture catches them just right. They fruited out in the springtime. They were stronger than the *muscaria* but were without the voluminous folklore that came with their red cousins.

For about two weeks he'd given me several small doses, then one evening he gave me about six large ones with water. I lost track of everything in about an hour. Then I found myself in a sea of entities that appeared to be only half-conscious almost eyeball nodes, perhaps former life holders, I didn't know. It was an awful subliminal place, greys and brown and blacks configured a half-lit landscape; I didn't know how I got there, and I didn't know for sure I was not one of them. It was a terrifying experience completely unconnected to a small cabin in Southern Oregon and any reality I had ever known, and the looming premonition that I would always be there was quite overwhelming as the lack of consciousness of time made me unsure of the fact that perhaps I had always been there.

Then, suddenly I fell from somewhere in this bad realm and I came back into my body, falling from a distance outside and briefly I saw my body lying on top of a bed. Then I suddenly consciously came to rest with my eyes wide open, but I was still terrified. I went down a ladder from this loft, hit the ground and did judo rolls across the carpet and out to the porch, then halfway around the house, and then I stood up screaming at the top of my lungs. The rest of the evening went by very pleasantly, or I probably never would have tried the mushroom again.

Not long after that, I came over one morning for coffee, and Pete fed me six dried pancake-size mushrooms as I walked in the door. I took them with a lot of water and then I went up on his roof and about an hour later he came up and gave me five more with water, I laid down and looked at the forest, took in the madrone trees and Douglas fir over Pete's house and, though slightly nauseous, I began to get extremely high, I moved slowly off the roof on a ladder.

I came down and made my way around his house and out to a postage-stamp-size lawn of about hundred square feet that was adjacent his house, and then down a path, beside his driveway and a small pond he'd made, with a pole bridge arcing over the top with transplanted river iris in the bank where a spring fed. I continued up the path where there were a number of Washington Lilies (*Lilium washingtonianum*), whose trumpet-shaped white flowers on stems five to six feet tall will exude a fragrance that can waft fifty feet or more. These radiant lilies are named for Martha Washington and walking by this air-filled florescence in white flowers nodding, facing outward, pale-lavender on the outside and tiny purple spots on inside, with their tips slightly curved, I continued onward and into a stand of ponderosa pine with a black oak understory and with a few Douglas fir mixed in. It was late spring and now the air exuded a dry balsam smell from the fir and the volatile resin of the pine, blending with the smell of the Lilies I was still passing by.

I was about a hundred yards from Peter's cabin and suddenly there was a man walking ahead of me I'd not seen before. He slowed, I got closer, and I noticed the man wore a whitish grey robe. This area had been a small sanctuary for the 'sixties, 'seventies and now 'eighties counterculture for some time. To see a man dressed in a robe would not have been out of character here.

He turned around and I saw clearly this man was Jesus, and this at the time he did not at all seem out of place in any manner—I was glad to see Jesus. He turned, and I noticed a demeanor that was not one of annoyance, but it was as if he had been distracted by me, from some other more pressing intention, perhaps. He looked like a father who was going to deliver a necessary explanation for a too-inquisitive child. I had said nothing and yes there was seemingly white light when I got close, not unlike the lilies at the edge of this forest.

"I'm going to show you something." He said as he approached close, "I'm going to show you something that most people don't get to see until they die."

He then touched me on my forehead with the flat part of a right forefinger bent slightly inward. His hand making a half-fist, then suddenly inside me seemingly every atom, every molecule of every plant, and every rock, and every tree and every drop of water, the air, and the bright blue summer sky—became Love. I can only describe it as a base of experiential reality more real than anything I'd ever known or have known since. *Love* was very apparently the construct of reality itself. Love was everything and it was all-pervasive and all around me, and inside me as well, and it came upon me with a physical touch? We all have a tough time with this as the one overwhelming Truth.

I found myself on the ground, after what seemed a timeless expanse and breathing deeply, I looked and realized that Jesus had since departed. I staggered back to Pete's house where there were now three people sitting on his small lawn in the middle of the Oregon woods.

"All there is—is love!" I blurted out! Then I said it again. And I said it again. They were friends of Peter and laughed as I announced this over and over.

I told no one about the Jesus part of this story for about 35 years, and I do not think I was supposed to. During that time, and for a time afterwards, I did assume this was a drug induced phenomenon and surging of wild flows of serotonin but I did entertain the idea that it was a vision nonetheless (this phenomenon in the charismatic world is called an open vision). Then after my own subjective, yet extra-earthly, always unexpected sober encounters with this same Jesus continued—though none were as a Christophany as I've just described; eventually, I discounted naturalism as a notion that gets you through anything other than the day to day, as important as that is. The base construction of reality it seems, is something else.

I have concluded His presence is everything: He came to end all evil that is somehow resident on this planet, despite the fact that this has not happened yet—Love *is* all there is.

Doctors, Lawyers, and the Indian Chief

FRED SULLIVAN HAD A COUPLE BEERS AT one of his old bars and headed out to his pal Jack's in Sam's Valley, who had a double-wide on the Rogue River about ten miles from where Fred had grown up. A twenty-minute drive on I-5 and the north Medford exit past Witham's truck stop and down past the airport on Table Rock Road and there was a sense of destination that Fred felt he'd not sensed in a long time. When he passed Avenue "G" and White City and down over the hill to Tou Velle Bridge over the Rogue River, he could see them. It was comforting. The Two Table rocks, and the last of the afternoon rays of sun on top of flat mesas in the middle of the Rogue Valley appearing in the dusk. Fred pulled the Red Crummy in a pull-out at the gauging station and crossed traffic and got out to take it all in: the orchards still blooming in places and the base of the upper Table Rock, the rock wall of the upper Table Rock in the middle and the traffic across the bridge. He'd not been here for a while. He'd not hunted the upper Table Rock but had been all over the lower one and Black Butte, just to its north, a volcanic appurtenance that was timbered with oak savannahs all around. Fred had met Jack on a tree planting job in '78.

They'd been hunting together since then. Even the last three years Fred had squirreled away $600 each year for an out-of- state tag into Oregon to hunt with Jack and several other friends from his high school days, Westwood, Glistens, the Deck brothers and Little and Big George Slaughter.

A lawyer had owned the Bar the Gate Ranch for thirty years, a medical doctor had owned the Table Rock Ranch for half that time but leased it when it became a profound certainty, he could not see 40 patients a day and ramrod a cattle ranch. Yet the ranches encompassed the lowlands around the lower Table Rock and effectively locked out all hunting in the oak savannahs, that swept around the base of the volcanic tower that pushed up from the bowels of the Earth where magma is formed, before there were humans.

The lawyer hired most of it out, and then subdivided most of the ranch save the acres next to the river where he built his home and eventually leased out the rest of it. The land had been farmed since 1890 and the Indians had been gone for 40 years before that. There was a landing strip built on the upper table rock during the war years when the whole of Sam's Valley had been pretty much appropriated to basic training of GIs in preparation for invading Europe. The pill boxes were still there on Antioch Road south of the upper Table Rock; evidence of the ordnance that had been fired at them repeatedly to prepare an assault on Hitler's supermen could still be seen in the pockmarked concrete around each opening.

Still, Chief Sam, a ghost now, from time to time walks along the edge of the Lower Table Rock, looking across the valley to where the magic was spread. He was walking there that evening. He knows now where his people went wrong; he knows also what they were right about—it was their home.

He walks and talks to himself and the spirits that can listen, and has been reunited with all that was lost, but he is allowed an occasional wander in the fulcrum of the interweaving of spiritual and natural worlds that were never separate at all. His father disagreed with the French priest who came with the French trappers, and he had told him it was not really medicine they brought. They had powerful medicine, but it seemed apparent they were not wanting to trade. The medicine that they had worked some days quite well; on other days it was hidden like a serpent's tongue and spread death in every lodge. He likes to come back when the side of snow on Mt. McLoughlin diminishes to obvious angel wings to let men know the salmon have come past the Table Rocks.

The Chief sees the difference and chuckles in late dusk when the light of civilization ramps up the night sky that only had stars when his corporeal bare feet strode this rock. He marvels but counts himself lucky in Sam's father's quarrel with the trapper priest centered on this argument. Despite what he said, they had their fierce secrets too that they would not reveal to all of the women or white men. What they would not reveal and secreted in bravado was surprisingly, that honesty, is the best policy, kindness does no-one harm, and despite wars all men are brothers, and despite the story telling there is but one God, the Father Almighty, Creator of all things. Sam believed what the priest had told them about his Son, and in secret counsel at the cave of initiation they all decided to believe this, but to tell no one because they knew in their hearts these white men were thieves—perhaps even the priest.

When the war came, they had killed white people—you see the miners were killing them—it was war. But when the peace treaty came, they did not think the incident could ever turn out the way it did.

When dusk to night on these walks and the light comes on in the valley below, Chief Sam sings quietly above the pines and looks down at the river below. It is hard to call Chief Sam a ghost. All the rocks and many of the trees he touched are still there. The roads, the lakes, the fences, and farms, some of them old now, were not there.

Sam counted many of the rocks and a great number of trees his friends—and many of these friends were gone. When his flesh touched the earth, he knew from boyhood that heaven was apparent from earth, and his heart longed for this appearance. The War was essentially over after the treaty meeting between the two Table Rocks. The California miners were encamped there. The Oregon miners were there. The Indians came, and the parlay had it that at the signal all would lay down their arms and they would talk. The Indians and the California miners laid down their arms then the Oregon miners shot the Indians, or was it the California miners? Sam didn't think of it anymore. The story had been spun as a battle. Chief Sam thought of only beauty that still welled up in his afterlife soul when he saw this landscape and called it by name—the Table Rocks were where the world began.

It ended probably in Jacksonville, oh the bloody death march to the north finalized it, but it ended when Chief Sam's grandnephew, orphaned and adopted by the good white family in the wagon with red wheels, brought the lad into town. The family had come into Jacksonville for supplies, with the young Indian boy, dressed as they were dressed and one of the miners that had taken part in the battle rode in amongst them, grasped the lad by his britches, rode him to the gallows, and had him hung, as there was another hanging about to happen. "Exterminate them all!" the demon-like man screamed as he dragged the child to the gallows. It all really ended that day and the white folks had their valley, and their squalid lives, and their descendants fared only slightly better.

The river had been dammed where they speared salmon and Sam still could not fathom all the quilted holdings of separate ownerships but he liked the twinkling lights and he began to walk around the rock in a westward manner until the sun set and he disappeared. But not before he thought the dam should go—and something whispered that it would.

Fred drove the Red Crummy between the two Table Rocks as darkness descended and took a right on Highway 234. Fifteen years later the Gold Rey dam was removed, and the herd of elk came back into Sam's Valley after a 100-year absence, crossing the river again at the lower Table Rock.

A Woman's Voice

WELL REALIZE—HE'D ALREADY named the animals! I didn't really have anything to do. Yes, we did walk in the garden every evening. So, I must admit maybe I was bored, but the serpent was an intellectual and he made me laugh, and I was laughing when I tasted it. I wanted to change the names of some of the animals; I must admit I never asked if I could, neither of them said I couldn't. It just seemed like it was a bargain already made. Oh, he would do anything for me! And well, I didn't even know that he hadn't named all the animals. Didn't find that out until, well, after we were outside and some of these other animals seemed to be intent on eating us.

Oh, this surprised me! This thing called fear, but now I like eating meat! But now the earth is hard.

Though now, I'm not bored with him any more I must admit. He protects and takes care of me, but these children, oh if I didn't have him, as much as I love them, it would be impossible because he guides them into a place they can find as their own. Yet you know, I think someday one of them may kill the other? I cannot imagine this.

I do miss those walks when it was the presence of His love, was as constant as breathing. Now there are only times when I look at him and vaguely remember. Still he can be bad. Now he growls from time to time, and once after drinking he hit me. This was not like him, and I bled, and now I bleed regularly at the moon, and what have we done?

I killed the snake last week and afterwards I heard him laugh from the grove in the garden. We can't go there anymore, but then again maybe it was from the forest beyond. I'm afraid of that place. Anyway, I saw the snake again the next day, I know, I should've known there was something wrong with a talking snake—but then don't you know, I had no idea what wrong was?

Now I still know where there are flowers by a quiet pool. Perhaps I could go there and come back? If I leave him it will be dangerous. Perhaps tomorrow I'll go there for a short while and then come back. Oh, my heart breaks when he screams in the middle of the night!

COLOPHON:

The body text, titles of stories and drop caps of this book are the Adobe Garamond™ font family based upon the typefaces first created by the French printer Claude Garamond in the sixteenth century. This serif face was created by Robert Slimbach and released by Adobe in 1989; its italics are influenced by the designs of Garamond's assistant, Robert Granjon. The cover, spine and title page font is Broadway, a decorative typeface, perhaps the archetypal Art Deco typeface. The original face was designed by Morris Fuller Benton in 1927 for ATF as a capitals only display face. ———

CPSIA information can be obtained
at www.ICGtesting.com
Printed in the USA
LVHW072057011020
590086BV00003B/112

9 781678 004286